Richard Wil[

Mostyn Thomas
and the Big Rave

To Luc and Leo

Mostyn Thomas and the Big Rave
Published in Great Britain in 2018
by Graffeg Limited

Written by Richard Williams copyright © 2018.
Designed and produced by Graffeg Limited copyright
© 2018.

Graffeg Limited, 24 Stradey Park Business Centre,
Mwrwg Road, Llangennech, Llanelli,
Carmarthenshire SA14 8YP Wales UK
Tel 01554 824000 www.graffeg.com

Richard Williams is hereby identified as the author
of this work in accordance with section 77 of the
Copyrights, Designs and Patents Act 1988.

A CIP Catalogue record for this book is available from
the British Library.

ISBN 9781912654161

123456789

Richard Williams
Mostyn Thomas and the Big Rave

GRAFFEG

Contents

Prologue

Every morning, suspended in his harness, Trevor would pan across the ancient estuary of the Cleddau to the heads and out to the ocean. On a calm, clear day, the rising sun would beam through the clouds of mist that hung over the water like sleeping ghosts, then explode into the thousands of fibres and textures that existed on the shores.

On rough days, thundering swells smashed over the headland, the torrents of spray shimmering in the bright morning sun. To be a lone spectator peering down on this unforgiving natural arena made him tingle with life like nothing else.

It was early April, a Tuesday. Trevor always knew to expect a perilous day in the harness when scores of surfers with their boards bound tightly to their roofs went soldiering across the bridge just after first light.

Trevor sometimes wondered, from his position a hundred feet above the open estuary, what surfing must be like. He'd often go down to Newgale Sands with Janice after work in the summer for a picnic and watch the surfers. He envied the flow of tanned girls and boys coming and going in their camper vans, parking up, flirting, touching, care-free. They'd skip over the pebbles with their boards and paddle out into the corduroy ocean as the sun slowly descended over St Brides Bay.

To be out there, away from the safety of the shore, those fluid silhouettes bold against the fiery skies around them, seemed to Trevor to be the ultimate expression of freedom.

If he had his time again, Trevor thought he would be a surfer. It was too late to start now, though. Despite decades of physical strain, at sixty-two he was sailing into his twilight years quite painlessly, so he felt no regrets.

Lowering himself into position, Trevor felt the rear harness clips digging into his back and carefully placed his painting gun up on the underside ledge of the bridge. He reached around and fumbled blindly, untwisting the clips to relieve the pressure, then reclaimed the painting gun and began to rub the obstructed barrel with his puffed, leathery fingers.

A strong gust of wind rattled through the underside of the bridge, blowing Trevor into a sway. He tried to settle himself, but felt a rapid loosening in the harness. One of his clips had come undone. Within seconds he was slipping out of the seat.

He grabbed for the safety rope and missed. His left knee tried to buckle onto the seat fibres as his body was forced out of the harness. He grappled to cling on. The unsettled water a hundred feet below drew the realisation that in a few seconds he would hit its surface.

He began to scream, but the swirling wind, thrashing rain and rumbling traffic on the bridge above smothered his cries. He spun around, scissor-kicking in desperation.

Finally, his hands left the rope.

The fall mangled Trevor, his body driven down into the cold water, the oxygen sucked from his lungs. He surfaced, flailing to stay afloat until a trickle of air could flow into him. His tool belt began to sink him like an anchor as he shook and contorted and managed to free himself.

A small sand bar was visible in the distance and he slashed towards it. He thought of Janice, of his two boys, Jethro and Jac, repeated the last words he'd said to Jethro that morning. 'I'm so sorry, boy. I didn't mean it.' He replayed the image of his son leaving the house with his head bowed, without saying goodbye.

Within a minute, he rapidly lost power. The muscles in his upper arms burned trying to keep momentum. Sodden layers of clothing were pulling him down. He stopped and turned onto his back to catch his breath. Cast around him was his bridge, majestic with its new coat of paint. He rolled back onto his front. He had to keep moving.

Every stroke was crucial. Dark thoughts flooded his mind. Would he sink and disappear, leaving Janice and the boys eternally searching? Or would he float, bloat and wash up stinking on the beach of the Jolly Sailor to a vigil of seagulls?

He felt his body tingling. There was a warmth now. He became more at ease in the water, kept moving toward the shore. Just a couple hundred yards. His will grew. Trevor stabbed down with his feet, searching for ground. He found it. The last fifty yards would be a wade in the deep salty mud to the bank of the estuary.

Trevor fell forward, face down in the shallows and crawled the final distance onto the sand. He'd made it.

He gazed across the small beach, regaining his breath, and saw a fat tabby cat staring at him from the top of a wall. The water began to dissipate from his body and the cold stabilised. He felt dead and alive in equal measures.

In the moments afterward, Trevor convinced himself that today was a divine rattling for him to change his ways. He would never be afraid again. Fear had buried most of his aspirations, all through his life. But now everything was clear. From this moment forward would be a new beginning. He couldn't wait to get home to give Janice the good news.

A pain shot up Trevor's arm and his chest tightened. His eyes burst open. He looked up at the bridge, now blurred, his world darkening. He felt coarse sand in the corner of his lips and moved instinctively to swipe it, but his heart stopped and he swiftly passed away.

The tabby cat wandered over and sat on Trevor's warm back and cleansed itself until the old man's body went cold.

Part I
Chapter 1

'Good afternoon, Mr Thomas. How are you today?'

'Aye, not so bad thanks, Jane. Just bloody overdressed again. Dew, dew, look at me sweating here.' Mostyn pinched the collar of his shirt and wafted the damp heat out of his chest.

'Yes, it's close, isn't it?'

'Aye, almost touching, girl. So what's the Kaiser's mood like today?'

Jane laughed. 'Oh, the usual.'

'Shit.'

'Come on.' Jane winked and waved him forward affectionately. 'He's just going through your file now.'

Mostyn took off his cap as he followed Jane down the silent corridor and into Mr Price's office.

The room had faint scents of cold cigarette and lavender, and the metal blinds had a sickly off-yellow tint. Mostyn noticed the undernourished cheese plant in the far corner of the room and wondered how Mr Price could fail to maintain it.

'Hello there, Mostyn,' said Mr Price as he breezed into the office, arm extended for his customary strong and uncomfortably long handshake. Mostyn always considered this to solidify rather than break the ice between them. 'Take a seat, please. Can Jane fix you a glass of water now?'

'Aye, please, that would be lovely,' said Mostyn.

Mr Price settled in his chair and fumbled for a pen. He grabbed each side of the desk, rolled himself up close, then jolted his arms up and forward in mid-air, like he'd just received a shock of electric current, only to settle his sleeves. He aligned his notepad, slid his glasses back up his nose with his right index finger, placed both elbows on the desk, resting his chin on his clenched fists, and finally grinned as he locked eyes with Mostyn, who was mesmerised by the entire performance.

Jane put the glass of water on the desk, smiled at Mostyn and left the room, closing the door behind her. Mostyn picked up the glass and took a long swallow.

'So, how's it going, Mostyn?'

'Aye, not so bad, Mr Price.'

'Good. Good. I hope you're giving yourself a bit of time off now the cattle are out. Have you started the second cut of silage yet? The grass seems lovely out Clarbeston way with all these long periods of sun and rain.'

'Well, I've been trying, Mr Price, but there's always a gate to mend or feet to do. The lanes were full of stones this spring after all that ice we had, so a lot of the animals are hobbling around in need of a trim. But the weather has been good, considering, so the silage and barley are looking healthy, that's a big relief. Let's just hope this weather holds up now till after the County Show.'

Mr Price smiled and studied Mostyn's face for a short moment. His cleft lip had become less noticeable with age and his thick grey hair remained perfectly side-parted, with boyish curls that rose up just under his earlobes. His eyes shone with a proud light and a resilient kindness. They could have belonged to an innocent adolescent trapped inside the ageing, wrinkled face of a troubled man who'd toiled alone in the elements for a lifetime. The wilt of his collar gave away his steady contraction into old age. Mr Price wondered how this solitary farmer would survive through his final years.

'Good, good,' said Mr Price.

Dust drifted through the hot afternoon sunrays as Mostyn took off his cardigan.

'So, what can I do for you today, Mostyn?'

Mostyn shuffled up in his chair and took another sip of water. The sweat that dampened his armpits was now blotting the front of his shirt. 'Well, things are still a bit tight. I'm not really getting anywhere, as you can probably see,' he said, pointing at the open file in front of Mr Price.

Mr Price nodded respectfully.

Mostyn drew a deep breath. 'So I think I need to expand.'

Mr Price's eyes widened. He eased back in his chair, folding his arms, thoughts brewing.

'I'd just like to widen and deepen the slurry pit so I can look for more head of cattle by the end of the year. I'm full to the brim now, even overflowing after a few days of solid rai—'

'Mostyn,' Mr Price interjected, 'are you seriously planning on asking the bank for another loan?'

'Yes, Mr Price.'

'For heaven's sake. Don't you realise you've missed your last nine overdraft repayments? And the loan for the cubicles, don't forget that. Look.' Mr Price's limp finger tapped on the spreadsheet as he rotated it for Mostyn to see, but Mostyn could see nothing. Such requests had just been formalities since his first loan back in 1971. He swallowed the last fingers of water, searching for a response.

Mr Price swivelled back and fore, slowly rolling his fingertips on the blotter of his desk.

'Look, Mostyn, let me spell it out.' Mr Price wiggled upright in his chair. He placed both elbows abreast on the table, brought his hands together in a prayer-like motion and began tapping his lower lip, his nose twitching. 'I've spent years fighting with Cardiff to keep small family farms afloat, all over the county. But due to all the current issues, the bank has a new policy that blocks further financing for farms that are not able to pay their overdrafts and loan repayments. And as I've just explained, Mostyn, you fall into that category.'

Mostyn took in a new and distant coldness in Mr Price's face. His mind raced for a solution. He could always sell land, but that would scupper his expansion plans. And the takings for the next lot of cattle going in a couple of weeks were already earmarked to cover overdue feed and vet bills. It would be another four months until the next lot of bullocks were ready.

'I'll find a solution, Mr Price. I've got a few score of cattle ready now in the next few weeks. If prices don't drop, I should be alright.'

Mr Price nodded again, calmly, knowingly.

It was a warm mid-summer's evening, so still he could hear the lazy squawk of the jackdaws nesting in the half-dead oak tree above the slurry pit, two hundred yards from the house.

'Enjoy tonight now, boy,' whispered Colwyn, carefully knotting his tie in the bathroom mirror. Staring into his reflection, that familiar blackness began to creep around his face and hollow out his eyes.

Cars flowed into the yard, and it soon became clear that just about the entire parish of Little Emlyn had come to celebrate Colwyn's sixty-fifth birthday. Ruth was thrilled to see the smile she'd loved for the past thirty-eight years return.

As the house swelled, Colwyn analysed the crowd, unsure, even in this close community, what some of his neighbours really thought of him after all these years. He was sure Tracy from the Corner House had held a grudge since he failed to attend her brother's funeral a few years back. There was Mervyn from the village – Colwyn had not spoken to him in over a year, since the chapel deacons voted to keep Mr Brown in as minister (Merv had led the attempted revolt to oust him for Gwyn Phillips, the retired schoolmaster). Even Carl Hancock, who two years previously had taken offence to Colwyn's playful mocking in the mart about his decision to trade in his cows for ostriches, turned up in a brand-new Range Rover.

All three made their way over to Colwyn even before the Bucks Fizz had all gone and wished him a happy birthday, all genuinely privileged to have been invited to celebrate with him.

The dancing started at 9pm. Colwyn was first onto the dining room dance floor, which he could see astonished and delighted his closest friends. He was usually the last man to dance at the Hunt Ball, and at weddings he was always found at the furthest point from the disco, in a quiet room, with a tumbler of whisky, talking about milk, cattle and barley prices.

What began as a stiff little jig soon loosened to some unusual moves that had those watching creased up with laughter. He continued, undeterred, with his eyes half-closed and a tongue-in-cheek smile as the village girls soon joined him, placing their handbags and shoes in a pile on the floor.

Colwyn could see Mostyn looking at him oddly from the corner of the dining room and strolled over.

'Alright, Most?'

'Aye, I'm alright, John Travolta. You?' asked Mostyn, eyebrows raised.

'Course, boyo, couldn't be better. Like my dancing, then?'

'Aye. Not kift at all, boy. Honest.' Mostyn smirked.

'Chopsy bugger,' said Colwyn. 'Lovely to see such a good turnout.'

'Aye. Tis. So how did it go with Mr Price?' asked Mostyn.

'Jesus, Most, it's my bloody sixty-fifth, man! I'll come over Monday and fill you in then.'

'Aye, no bother,' said Mostyn. 'Sorry, boy. Just you remember that whatever happens, we'll be fine, Col. We're in this together. I saw him yesterday, and I'm up to my nuts in shit as well. I'll tell you about it on Monday. Just make sure we stay honest with each other. No bullshit. You got that?'

'Aye, Most,' said Colwyn.

'Anyway, you enjoy your birthday tonight now, boy. It's great to see everyone here.'

Mostyn had spotted Shifty in the kitchen and weaved his way towards him. He had known Shifty for the past twelve years, since he'd moved to the Welsh coast from Liverpool to set up his second-hand car garage. The last time Mostyn went looking to buy a little run-around, Shifty took him into his cabin and told him straight, 'Sorry, Mostyn, I wouldn't sell you any of these cars I've got here at the moment, mate.'

Since that day, Mostyn had held Shifty in the highest regard and considered him a friend. This was why he asked Shifty if he could borrow some money.

'I wish I could, mate, but with all youse farmers struggling, things have slowed right down for me too, pal. No one's got any money these days. It's fucking shite, Most, it really is. The only person I know of who's still giving out loans is the Growler.'

'The Growler?'

'Aye, he's that moneylender. You must have heard of him?'

Mostyn shook his head blankly.

'Very mysterious, but he's from around here somewhere. No one's ever met him. They say his real name's Beverley, and that's why he came up with the Growler.' Shifty grinned.

'How come no one's ever met him?' asked Mostyn.

'Well, he's got this "representative". Weird Head, he's called, who takes care of all his business. Gnarly bastard, but seems nice enough if you don't get on the wrong side of him.'

'Weird Head?' asked Mostyn, smirking.

'Aye, Weird Head. Funny as fuck, I know. But when you see him, Most, you'll see why, and you won't fucking laugh at him, I promise you.'

'But as long as loans are paid back, they don't mess about with people, do they?' asked Mostyn.

'No, no, I'm sure you'd be fine. He's been operating around here for years. If they fucked people over, they wouldn't last long in the business. It's too small a community for that.'

Mostyn nodded, half-reassured. 'So how can I get to speak to this Weird Head then?'

'He drinks down the Mariners. He's always there when I go for a pint on Fridays between five and seven-ish. Just go up to him and tell him you spoke to me. But be a bit discreet – there's no contracts, invoices, or any of that shit. Be aware they work on a gentleman's agreement. You can't fuck about with these people, Mostyn. Only borrow if you can pay back quite quickly, OK?'

'Aye, no fear for that, boyo. I could always sell something if need be.'

The phone rang at 7.18am. Mostyn picked it up, still in a stupor from the party. He thought he'd only just gone to bed.

'Hello?'

'Hello, Mr Thomas. It's Giles Noot here from Thornhill Farm, next door. Sorry to bother you so early, old chap, but I think some of your cattle have escaped and wandered over to my house and destroyed my fucking lawn.'

Giles was right – the lawn was a mess, and the ten or so cattle were now leisurely looting any morsels of edible vegetation available to them around the beautifully restored farmhouse. Mostyn cringed when he saw the flowerbeds obliterated, petals strewn across the floor. Giles came out with his children, Poppy and Sam, in his arms. They were young, around three and one, dressed like they'd just stepped off the cover of a glossy family magazine and both looking very unhappy.

'Hello, Giles. Hello, kids. Sorry about all this. I'll get these beasts out of here in no time,' said Mostyn.

Giles stared at him, expressionless.

'Hey up! Get out of it! C'mon, c'mon,' yelled Mostyn, over and over, waving his arms and lashing the cattle with a stick.

The children squirmed.

'Are you going to compensate me for this mess, Mr Thomas?'

'Excuse me? What do you mean?' asked Mostyn.

'What do you mean, "what do you mean?" Have you not heard of the word compensation before in Pembrokeshire? This lawn cost me nearly two thousand pounds to returf.'

'I have, Giles, but I'm sorry, this happens quite a lot in these parts, as I'm sure it does in other rural parts of the country. Once I get these animals back in, I'll come around and fix up the lawn. It won't take me long.'

'Good,' said Giles.

Mostyn turned, rolled his eyes and continued to round up his cattle.

He ushered the last of the animals back into his field, locked the gate and began to walk back down to Giles's house to try and calm relations. The thought of not getting on with a neighbour, even a rude English one, was something Mostyn wanted to avoid.

A 4x4 pulled into the lane and tore down towards the house. Brown dust clouds billowed skywards in its wake. Imogen, Giles's wife, jumped out, grabbed her groceries and walked briskly towards the back door.

'Giles, terrible news at the farmers' market this morning, dear. Apparently some old farmer killed himself last night, on his sixty-fifth birthday. Not far from here too. His wife threw a big party for him, then he hung himself in the shed straight after. Selfish old fool. Can you imagine?'

Giles felt a presence. There was Mostyn, across the backyard, staring squarely at Imogen. His face had dropped and he was blinking furiously. He knew she was talking about Colwyn, and his instinct told him it was true.

Mostyn put his hand out and reached for the nearest fence post to steady himself. 'I could have stopped him,' he whispered, nausea rising from his stomach. 'Why did I bloody listen to him?'

'Hello. Mr Thomas from next door, is it?' Imogen said softly, not knowing what else to say.

Mostyn gathered his thoughts as the stoicism schooled into him by his father kicked in and dampened his guilt. He blew his nose, a smokescreen to dry his eyes, and raised his head. 'Yes, Mrs Noot, it is. And that selfish old fool was my best friend, Colwyn.' He took a deep breath and felt a cool determination to put his new neighbours in order. 'We first met in Sunday school when we were three years old, back in the thirties. Went to school together, just down there. It's the village hall now. Back in those days, it was called the North School. We lived through the war together, me and Col – we thought it was just one big adventure. We were just kids. We were lucky living out here. We spent our teenage years playing cowboys and Indians in those woods just there, going to dances in town, courting young ladies. We were both taken out of school at fifteen to come home and work the land. It's been a hard life, but the life we lived after the war up until recently was quite something that I can't explain to you, Mrs Noot. We had it all – community, family, a business that worked and rewarded us just enough for us to carry on.'

He paused.

Giles and Imogen were silent.

'But then we had milk quotas, open markets, butter from France, lamb from New Zealand. New Zealand! And both cheaper than our butter and our lamb. Then BSE arrived. You may know that most of the farms around Little Emlyn rear beef, Mrs Noot. The land's rich but difficult to cultivate crops on, what with the hills, valleys and woodlands. It's perfect for grazing, though, and our beef is some of the best you will ever taste, what with the quality of the soil and the fresh Atlantic air blowing in. But now this mad cow disease is wiping out our industry. Maybe not forever, but for small farmers like myself and Col, too old to move with the times, it's finished. Well, it's certainly finished for Col.'

Mostyn dropped his head and kicked a stone that was lying by his foot. It pinged through the tension, crashing into a galvanised fence post at the end of the old milking parlour across the yard.

Imogen took a step towards him. Mostyn put his hand up. 'It's OK, Mrs Noot. You weren't to know I was standing here, and you don't know us. I'll be back sometime in the week to patch up your lawn.'

Giles spoke up, 'No, no, Mr Thomas, it's fine, really. I'm so sorry for my behaviour this morning. I was just shocked when I pulled up the kitchen blinds and saw all those cattle. It's just a patch of bloody grass. Please, don't worry about it, it's fine.'

Mostyn raised his cap and looked them both in the face momentarily. He could see they were good people. He picked up his stick and walked back home across the fields, his eyes sweeping the grass, searching for Col's motives. It just didn't add up. His lower lip began to quiver – he could already feel the coffin rope slipping from his hands.

'Pint of shandy and a Crunchie please, love.'

This was Mostyn's first visit to the Mariners in about four years. Nothing had changed. He was sure that was the same near-empty bottle of Blue Curacao at the back of the spirit shelf that poisoned him on Christmas Eve, 1989.

He took his pint and settled at the side of the bar overlooking the beach. It was late Friday afternoon and the bar began to fill with tradesmen clocking off after the week's work.

Just as he finished poking his Crunchie wrapper into a tiny ball in his fist, he spotted Weird Head. It had to be him. His head looked odd – a huge forehead with a hairline receding back to the middle of his crown. He had short, shaved black hair and eyes that were small and very close together. His nose was bulbous with gaping nostrils, and his small mouth looked like it had been half drawn, like an old purse. His bottom jaw stuck out and his chin was as long as his forehead was high. Mostyn thought that if his eyes and mouth were twice the size, he'd probably look all right, but they weren't.

It took Mostyn three pints to approach him. He was sitting alone next to the empty fireplace reading the week's local news in the *Western Telegraph*.

'Excuse me, sir, sorry to bother you. I've been recommended by my friend Shifty up at Little Emlyn Motors to come and speak to you. My name is Mostyn.' He cautiously offered his hand.

Weird Head frowned for a moment. 'Hello, Mostyn. Weird Head.' They shook firmly. 'Nice to meet you. How's that Scouse cowboy doing these days?'

Mostyn tittered. 'Aye, he's not so bad. Still moaning about how bad business is. Still blaming us farmers for all his troubles.'

'He's such a little fucker, old Shifty, but he's alright. What can I do for you, Mostyn?'

Mostyn sat down opposite Weird Head and dragged his chair nervously across the slate floor, making sure there was no audience.

'Well, if the truth be told, I'm in a temporary spot of financial trouble, Mr Weird, er...' Mostyn froze.

'It's fine, Mostyn. Everyone calls me Weird Head,' he said, pointing to his head and flashing a smile.

By God you're ugly, thought Mostyn. 'Yes, well, as you may know, a lot of us small farmers are struggling at the moment, and I've got a little bit of a gap to fill with some overdue expenses I need to pay before my next lot of cattle go at the end of August.' This was a lie. Mostyn knew those funds were already spent. 'Would you be interested in lending me quite a few thousand pounds, short term of course, just to get me through?'

'Own your farm, do you, Mostyn? Have a good base of assets should you need them?' asked Weird Head, polite and professional.

'Aye, no worry for that. I've got a hundred and thirty-five acres and lots of machinery. All mine, bought and paid for. I don't see it ever getting to the point of having to sell any of those,' said Mostyn, confidently.

'Of course,' said Weird Head, 'but it's good to be careful, Mostyn. You don't want to risk losing everything you've ever worked for now, do you? How much would you be looking to borrow?'

'Not too sure. I'll need to check my accounts, but maybe something in the region of ten to twenty thousand pounds, if you were kind enough to lend such an amount.' Mostyn gnawed his left thumbnail rampantly as Weird Head considered his request.

'OK, Mostyn, I'll speak to the gaffer and see what he says. I don't see there being any problem. I'll just need a few more details from you.'

Weird Head asked Mostyn a number of not unusual questions about his finances and assets and they parted company.

Mostyn joined an old friend, Griff Harries, at the bar. As the beer went down, Mostyn's anxiety sank with it. He felt sure this loan would put him back on track.

He went to the toilet, unzipped his fly, rested his head on the pipe above the urinal and closed his eyes. His lungs filled with the stench of bleach and urine.

Mostyn's eyes popped open. A familiar voice outside was becoming increasingly loud and aggressive.

'You've got till noon Monday. If you don't turn up, I'm going to rip your fucking throat out, you understand me, boy? My gaffer don't like late payments, so sort it out, otherwise I will make your life a living hell. You fucking got that?'

Mostyn dashed into the cubicle, feeling the last dribble of piss seep into his trousers. He sat down to dry himself. A man entered the toilets, breathing heavily, and ran the tap. Mostyn cautiously moved his head in line with the gap in the cubicle door and saw the back of the man. He was wearing a tatty old tweed suit and was curled over the sink, snivelling. There was blood on the hand towels, but he couldn't see the man's face.

He was sure it was a farmer.

Chapter 2

The ship lurched from side to side and Jethro wanted to get off. He didn't remember boarding the boat and was confused. He stood up and began walking sideways towards the toilets. His eyes swayed with the motion of the sea. He approached a group of scantily clad girls at the side of the dance floor, all with tiny waistlines and slender faces, like prizewinning cats.

'Excuse me,' he said to the girl with glitter on her cheeks. He paused, momentarily forgetting his question. 'How do we get off this thing?'

'Eh? What you on about, mate?' yelled one girl, cutting through the loud music.

'I want to get off the boat. I don't like it.'

'What you on about? You look fucked.'

'I want to get off. I reckon it's gonna sink. Seriously, it's all over the place. There's too many people on here.'

The tall girl with curly red hair and a delicious splattering of freckles seized Jethro's shoulders and pulled him towards her. 'Mate,' she yelled into Jethro's face, with a one-sided smile. Jethro's eyelids catapulted open and their eyes met. 'You're off your tits. We're in Chequers! In Penally. Remember? You sure you're OK?'

Jethro stooped towards her, frowning. His eyes looked like two distant black holes.

'Here, have some water.' She passed her bottle and Jethro took a sip. 'Seriously, man, don't take any more pills.'

Jethro turned his head and fixed his eyes on the blackness behind the girls. The girls rolled their eyes, smirked and walked away.

Jethro began to slide deeper into his trip. He watched from the shadows of the club where all of the deals took place. Normally he would skit in and out of this dark corner for his ecstasy warily. But at this moment, he felt untouchable, the captain of his ship, feasting in his psychedelic universe of pulsating beats, flashing lights, colours and beautiful young people.

He spotted a bouncer with a tattoo down one side of his neck. Jethro didn't like bouncers. They were vicious, and connected to the dealers. Confiscated drugs were often seen being slipped back to the peddlers from Swansea and Ammanford for resale. Jethro couldn't help staring at the bouncer, and soon the bouncer stared right back at him.

Jethro's mind began to slide again. To his horror, the bouncer's face began to move, wobble, then twist and finally distort into what looked like a big fuzzy black tennis ball. Jethro was transfixed. He took one step towards the bouncer and his tennis ball head began to manifest into something different. Worms began dripping off his face and giant bees swarmed violently around the bouncer's head. As the rapid metamorphosis progressed, Jethro's jaw dropped and his eyes widened when the bouncer's head revealed its second incarnation: the head of a Gamorrean guard, one of the servants to the crime lord Jabba the Hut. Half-pig, half-monster, green, with four menacing tusks protruding from his oversized jaw and an ugly oversized snout that dripped with thick translucent slime.

The guard held Jethro's stare and looked to mumble words in his direction. It was time for Jethro to leave. He turned around and made his way towards the grand staircase that led up to the nightclub balcony, but two bouncers were either side of the stairway on the bottom step. Their heads too became heads of Gamorrean guards and they both looked squarely at Jethro. They had big axes, so there was no way Jethro was getting past to alert his friend Biscuits. He didn't know what to do. He turned again and dissipated into the middle of the dance floor. His mouth tremored and his teeth began to chatter. He dropped his head, closed his eyes, and whispered to himself over and over, 'This is not real.'

Jethro was awoken by a slow rumble of thunder. He didn't dare to move. He kept his head still while his eyes ping-ponged around the room. He knew that if he shifted more than an inch, in any direction, the damp chill of the early morning would break the fragile seal of warmth. The hallucinations continued, but with less intensity. The flowers on the curtains swayed slowly and the walls gurgled. He looked down at the back of his hands and screwed up his face, saw the worn scaly skin of a reptile and his thick blue veins clogged with gloopy blood, the by-product of last night's activities.

The room was shot through with a soft orange glow. Dust filled the air. The house was abandoned, but with most of its furniture still in its place, bathed in layers of ash-like dust, dripping in cobwebs.

Jethro thought of Miss Havisham's house, and wondered if a ghostly old lady still wandered the creaky floorboards of this forgotten rural home.

Rain began to lash down as Jethro rested his head back on the floor in his mind-bent slumber. He wondered who had lived in this house, what caused them to abandon it with all of their belongings. Cushions were still on the sofa and a children's book was open on the floor between him and the dresser. It must have been a sudden event of despair; Jethro felt it too.

Jethro needed to smoke. He pulled himself up and immediately felt the cold and the damp. He was thin and pale, with a pretty, narcotic-chiselled face. The pallor of his skin was made whiter by the jet-black hair that hung in shards across his forehead and by the shadows smudged underneath his eyes.

He held onto the back of a chair until his blood had settled then reached for his tobacco. He rolled a cigarette, smoking it as he drifted from room to room. He came to the kitchen, saw the Aga set timelessly under the giant farmhouse chimney. The oak beam supporting the chimney breast drew Jethro towards it and he ran his cold fingers along its ancient grains.

There was a small cough. 'Morning, fuckface,' a voice quietly growled.

Jethro looked down. There was Biscuits, curled up at the base of the Aga, his mop of hair covering half of his face. 'What you doing there?'

'What do you mean? Sleeping, you knob. What do you think?'

'Why there?'

'Why not?'

'Cos that cosy Aga has been off for years. Keeping you warm, is it?'

'You're such a fucking comedian. Make us a coffee.'

'Yeah. That would be nice. How the hell did we end up here, Biscuits?'

'I have no idea. I'm still tripping my nads off, aren't you? Jesus. I won't even tell you some of the things that have gone through my head in the past few hours, they're just not right. It's these mountains, man. I'm sure there's something about them.'

'I know what you mean,' said Jethro, quietly and seriously. 'I've just been in Chequers via a boat party. Fuck me. I'm alright now, I think. Just freezing my balls off.'

Jethro walked to the kitchen window and assessed the wild escarpment that ran from the plains all around the house up to the top ridges of the Preseli Hills, just a mile or so in front of him.

'Wow, that is fucking beautiful, Biscuits. Look at this view, man.' Jethro paused for a moment to absorb the vista, smudged with huge blobs of mist and clouds so low you could almost blow them away. 'The Preselis looming over us in all their desolate glory. I think you're right that there's magic in them hills, boy. When I die, you can burn me to Gat décor, 'Passion'. The original, not that new remix with the stupid fucking acapella over the top. Then sling my ashes from the top of that ridge up there, OK?' Jethro pointed and made sure Biscuits clocked the ridge and nodded.

'Yeah, J, no worries, I'll do that,' said Biscuits, half-listening while he pulled his arms inside his red sweater to keep warm.

'Just make sure the wind is coming from the south-west so my ashes settle on these plains...then I'll be free...for eternity! Ha, ha, ha!'

'Jesus, Jethro, will you stop going on about death, man. You never stop. You're fucking nineteen years old. You haven't even passed your driving test. When you do, then you'll be free. Plus, you still haven't seen Sasha, you've only shagged one bird and you've never even been to France. You've got it all to fucking do, pal. Seriously, if your old man could hear you, he'd foot you in the arse.'

'Well he's not, is he?'

'No, he's not, but come on, J, he's probably looking down on you now, and if he'd heard the way you're talking, I'm sure he'd have given you a heavenly bitch slap by now.'

A gentle tremor of thunder rolled across the distant hills.

'See, told you so!' exclaimed Biscuits. 'Old Trevor is farting feathers in heaven cos his eldest son is still harping on about death when he's got everything to live for and his whole life ahead of him.'

'OK, OK, change the fucking subject. You're right. I need to sort my head out. I know everything's fine, but these thoughts, man. They're a bastard.'

They sat in silence for a few minutes sharing another roll-up, watching the smoke as it coiled upwards and filled the old room.

'This place is mental,' said Jethro. 'Everything is still here. Look.' He pointed to the kitchen table and the three empty milk bottles, a dust-caked magazine with the words *Radio Times* faintly visible, and a rose-patterned teapot. He picked up the magazine and gently blew the dust away. 'November 1984,' he whispered, as if he'd just unearthed treasure. 'Ten fucking years this place has been empty. Jesus.'

Biscuits remained silent.

Jethro swung his finger to the sink, which still had plates on the draining rack, and raised his eyebrows at Biscuits for approval.

'Dry now, are they?'

'What do you think happened? Must have been something really bad, no? You just don't get up one day and decide to leave your life and belongings, especially on a farm this remote. What do you think happened to all the animals?'

'Dunno,' said Biscuits. 'Have you got any weed left?'

Biscuits was a boy of few words, but he never minced them. He had had a tough upbringing in Neyland, a town, of sorts, perched on the northern banks of the Cleddau estuary. The town had fallen from glory since the days of its founding as a transatlantic terminal for the largest ships of the nineteenth century by Isambard Kingdom Brunel, who extended the Great Western Railway to meet the port. Neyland enjoyed a good century of prosperity, but now its most notable assets were a well-stocked Spar, a renowned chippy and Chinese, and the hardest women in Pembrokeshire.

There were four general paths of destiny laid out for the young men of the town. The first – onto the rugby field, second – into the armed forces, third – to the oil refineries, and the fourth – straight to prison.

Biscuits was a misfit. His father, Dean, was a big man and an even bigger drinker. His face, like his stomach, was bloated. His nose was red, wide and bumpy, and his blond, centre-parted mullet was always tucked behind his tiny pinned-back ears. He was known for his stamina in work and play, and for his incapacity to remain civil when drunk. Not many people liked Dean, but no one in Neyland would ever challenge him.

Dean worked as a fitter on oil refinery shut-downs all over the country. He'd be away for several months at a time, working twelve-hour days. He'd then come home, spending most of his money on accessories for his ever-changing 4x4 Ford Sierras. The rest was spent on lager, chips and takeaway Chinese food. Aside from paying the rent, little was given to the family, and Dean made it clear to them how hard it was to work twelve-hour days back to back for weeks, even months, on end.

Dean's wife, Connie, had three jobs: working as a dinner lady in Neyland Primary School in the mornings and lunchtimes, changing beds in Withybush hospital in the afternoons, and working two nights a week in Neyland chip shop, with Janice, Jethro's mother. It was tough, but the family got by, especially when Dean was not around.

Biscuits and his brothers, Mark and Paul, were quite close, but Dean tried his best to divide them. He favoured Mark and Paul as they played rugby for the local youth teams, which gave Dean the opportunity to go to the athletic club every Saturday and spend the entire day drinking gallons of lager, embarrassing his sons, and irritating most of the men of the town.

Biscuits hated sport. Aside from a bit of reading about history and culture, the only thing he had ever loved was music. His early teenage years revolved around the Top 40 on Sunday afternoons on Radio One. He lived for those three hours of music, taping the entire show on his small cassette recorder, then spending the next three days editing 'best-of' compilations for his friends and any girls he wanted to impress in class.

His friends knew his home life was not idyllic, as Connie and Dean were often heard screaming at each other in the background of the mixtapes. Biscuits was so used to these arguments that he rarely noticed.

Biscuits had discovered rave music and ecstasy with Jethro one summer's evening in 1991, at Chequers nightclub, near Tenby. The DJ, Pelham, weaved in The Prodigy's 'Charly' three times during the laser show, blowing Biscuits' mind to pieces. He never looked back. His miserable teenage years were brushed away by the tribal beats and spirit of family and togetherness of the rave and later the house music movements.

Despite being short, his cheeky, disarming smile and long wavy brown hair attracted no shortage of young ladies on the dance floors and he was optimistic about life for the first time in years.

But his father had noticed a change in him – weight loss, androgynous club gear and the 'bleepy drug music' that throbbed relentlessly from his bedroom. Dean began to humiliate him, calling him 'The Little Dancing Faggot' in front of his friends, even kicking him up the backside regularly when he saw him moping around the house. Aside from the insults, Dean had not bothered to ask Biscuits a single question about anything for the past three years. He sensed long ago that his youngest son was different, and decided two out of three was good enough.

Biscuits reciprocated the hands-off relationship. On the rare occasions the family sat around the dinner table, Biscuits felt invisible. Some days he wished his father were dead. He imagined stabbing him to death, and fantasised at the look of horror on his father's face as he gasped for his last breath. Every time Dean set off on a new job, Biscuits wished the minibus would never return.

'Fuck, the pills,' said Jethro.

'What?' said Biscuits.

'The fucking pills. And the cash.' Jethro frantically checked his pockets and stomped back to where he had slept, sweep-searching all around. 'They've all gone. Jesus, Biscuits, I'm fucked now. Properly fucking fucked. Jesus.' Jethro started tapping his head uncontrollably.

'Shit. Think, J, where did you last have them?'

'I don't know. I remember counting them when it was still daylight last night. I remember selling a few to the surfers and some to the hippies. That's it, Biscuits. I don't remember fuck all after that.'

Jethro continued to scan around the house, digging and digging into his empty pockets. 'Jesus. Why am I such a fucking loser? Two hundred and fifty pills on tick. Where the fuck am I going to find two grand? Ronnie's gonna cut me into pieces.'

'Don't be daft. Just tell him the truth – he'll be alright.'

'Are you fucking mental? He's the angriest bastard I've ever met. He drove a fucking JCB into Stewie Evans's house because he didn't pay up for a bag of pills only a few weeks ago. He's a fucking psycho. I may as well top myself now.'

'Stop it, J. Look, let's just get home and get some sleep. You can't think straight now.'

The dying pulses from the mushrooms lost their peculiar glow in a few heartbeats. Jethro started to shiver.

'Jethro, snap out of it, mate. We need to get home, now. Come on, we'll sort it out, I promise. Where are we? Do you have any idea?'

'We must be down past the cattle grids, Brynberian side,' said Jethro. 'I recognise that ridge. Foel Cwmcerwyn is just up over the top there somewhere. We're on the north side now.'

'Aye, alright, I'll follow you. Come on, let's go,' said Biscuits.

As they left the house through the back door, Biscuits noticed a light on in one of the sheds. 'That's weird,' he said. 'Look, there's a light on over there. Wait here and I'll go check it out.'

Biscuits shimmied his way across the waterlogged backyard,

reached the shed and slid open the big red wooden door.

'Holy fuck!' shouted Biscuits. 'Come and check this out, J.'

Jethro traversed his way across the yard, still shivering. Inside the shed was a trove of agricultural machinery.

'Look at all this shit!' exclaimed Biscuits. 'It must be worth thousands. Look – tractors, those big things, harvesters I think, balers, and look at all those fucking tools. There's a small fortune right there, Jethro.'

'So what?' asked Jethro.

'Well, we could lift some of this shit, sell it, and pay back Ronnie.'

'You must be joking,' said Jethro. 'What, then have some wacky Preseli's Texas chainsaw farmer after my knackers as well? You're off your head. Come on, let's get the fuck out of here.'

They walked around to the front of the farmhouse and headed down the boggy lane of the moor. A small murmuration of starlings fled the nearby woodland and the boys stopped in their tracks to watch the rhythm of the birds snaking like ink across the monochrome sky.

'Bit early for starlings,' said Jethro.

Biscuits wasn't listening. 'Why was the light on in that shed?'

'We must have gone in there last night when we were off it,' said Jethro.

'Oh, aye,' said Biscuits. 'That's a weird fucking set-up there,' he muttered to himself. He shivered too.

They came to the main road and walked in silence towards the dank, foggy hill pass above them. Jethro imagined he was ascending into hell. Just his luck.

A sheep lorry picked them up just before 11am and dropped them on the bypass just outside town.

'Oi, wanker, what the fuck happened to you last night?'

Jethro was rattled from his deep sleep and sat up in his bed. 'Hey, babe.'

'Don't you fucking "hey, babe" me, you prick. You left me and Lucy with all those fucking hippies last night. Where did you go?'

'Katie, I have no idea. I swear. Me and Biscuits woke up in this abandoned farmhouse on the moor between the cattle grids and Brynberian this morning. Honestly, how the fuck we ended up there I have no idea. I'm so, so sorry. It was those mushrooms. That old hippy, the one that looked a bit like Terry Nutkins, he made the brew. I knew it was strong, but hell fuckin' fire, it was mental. I've never tripped like that before.'

'Well that's fucking marvellous, Jethro, but you left us to those weirdos. They span us right out, and most of them were in their fifties and sixties. All out of it. They just wanted to get us fucked and get their stinking little old hands into our knickers. One of the fuckers fell into the fire pit and nearly burned to death. The screams were horrific. It was fucking madness trying to put the flames out on him.'

'Holy shit,' said Jethro, sitting up. 'I remember that screaming. Shit. I remember now. I remember Biscuits telling me someone was being stabbed. We panicked and legged it off into the fields. Shit.'

'You could smell his flesh burning.' Katie slipped back into the story, now calm and entranced.

Jethro could see she had been affected.

'That killed the party. The music stopped, and they were all wrapping him in wet cloths, like a fucking mummy, screaming. It got really weird then. Bad vibes and spun-out hippies, all off their tits. Blaming each other. Screaming at each other. It was primeval. So vicious as well. You could sense this deep-rooted contempt they all had for each other. Hatred. I know they were all off it, but it was clear as day. All this communal living and community shit they try and project onto everyone is a load of shit. Seriously. They're all a bunch of fucked-up, selfish loonies. Lost souls. Fucking evil, some of them. I wouldn't have pissed on any of them if more had caught fire.'

'Jesus, Katie, that's a bit harsh.'

'Harsh? Fucking harsh?' She turned her aggression directly towards Jethro, her dilated eyes framed by her fringed bob. 'Look at you. I guess I can expect you to be wanting to slit your wrists by about, let me see, teatime Tuesday, yeah?'

'Thanks, Katie. That's really nice.'

'Oh fuck off, Jethro. Don't start with all that puppy dog shit. Loser.'

'Stop.' He looked down and rubbed his hands anxiously between his knees. 'I lost all the pills as well.'

Katie threw her head up, laughing. Her eyes sparkled. 'What? All of them?'

'Yes. And all the cash from the ones I sold.'

'You fucking twat. That doesn't surprise me one bit. Ronnie's gonna be tamping beyond. You're dead! What the fuck are you gonna do, Jethro? Eh? What?'

'Why are you so fucking horrible?'

'Look, Jethro, I've just had enough. It's been fucking turmoil the whole time, except for the drugs. I know you lost your dad, but I'm sorry, you can't expect me to be sad forever with you. I never even met him.'

'Get out.' Jethro's voice stiffened. His dark eyes pierced fiercely back into hers.

She looked him up and down. 'Pleasure.' Jethro put his pillow over his head and sobbed. Katie's words repeated over and over in his head. He missed his dad. He still couldn't cope with the thought of never seeing him again. Holding him again. There was no goodbye, no last hug, no pat on the back. The last words his father said to him: 'I never thought I'd say this, Jethro, but you've turned out to be a loser. Waste of fucking space. Look at you, like a fucking zombie.'

Jethro knew he didn't mean it, was certain he'd regretted those parting words as he plummeted into the estuary.

Jethro sank deeper into the bed. He felt the same fear that had crushed him as a young boy, around seven years old, when he realised that he was not immortal, that one day he would die. His sobs that night had brought his father rushing into his bedroom to comfort him, to tell him that he didn't have to worry about that now, that he had a long and happy life ahead of him, that he would likely live to over one hundred years with doctors being so clever today and that heaven was an amazing place where he would be reunited with all of his family that had passed away before him.

Jethro began to wail. He couldn't swallow. He sank deeper still. He imagined Ronnie grabbing his throat, the hands of that vicious and crazy old criminal.

As the minutes turned into hours, Jethro could see no light.

Chapter 3

The head appeared out of nowhere, like a periscope. Not a breath of wind. A sea of glass, bitumen black under the hood of fog, so thick and bleak the diver had to squint to find the cliff face. He pulled off the mask and sucked the warm, moist air into his lungs. He made himself small, the holes of his nostrils bobbing quietly above the water as he panned the empty landscape. This desolate world made for good money. He began to stroke his way towards the cove. His load was heavy. He passed the rope from hand to hand, rotated onto his back and glided for a moment, then, as he sank, rolled back onto his front to repeat his self-taught technique.

He reached the shore.

The cove was severe. Narrow, but deep. Axed out of the land like a wedge from a giant oak. Its small beach was steep, strewn with sharp rocks and rounded pebbles along the tiny shoreline. Jetsam lay all around. A storm cove, like scores of others littered along the south-westerly facing cliffs of the Pembrokeshire coast. The perfect landing ground for the pirates and smugglers who commandeered these untamed secret inlets for centuries.

The diver emerged from the water, gave one last heave on the rope and his wiry frame buckled delicately onto the pebbles. He panted for air and ripped back his hood. Steam billowed from his head as he shook off the tank and tugged and stamped his way out of the wetsuit. He couldn't cool down. He edged back into the water, naked. The rushing coolness as he dived washed away his discomfort. He stood up, chest deep, closed his eyes and slid both hands tightly over his scalp, from his forehead to his neck, squeezing the creamy saltwater from his hair. It felt good.

He assessed the package. A rectangular block, tightly bound in reams of plastic. The biggest pick-up to date. Surely. He gathered his things, hoisted the block onto his shoulder and made his way up the steep cliff face. His calf muscles screamed. He focused – one foot, then the next – through the fog and the fading light.

The sun had just set by the time the diver pulled into the entrance of the smallholding, descending the bumpy lane towards the old stone house that overlooked the north coast of St Brides Bay. The horizon drew his gaze. The fog had lifted. Black and orange seams, as wide as the Earth, separated the ocean from the sky. A sharp crescent moon hung over Skomer Island. He scanned the sky again, orange, to blue, to black.

The car seemed to roll reluctantly into the yard, the slow cadence of crushed gravel under its tires sending the crows fleeing from their nests. The diver stepped out and looked around the yard. No vehicles. Just the shells of a Capri, up on blocks, and an Escort, its passenger door still open. Rusted skeletons, colonised with weeds.

He cleared his throat as he tugged on the mouthpiece of the CB radio. He flicked it out and his lips touched the small grill as his thumb sank the button. 'Breaker, Breaker to Candyman. You got your ears on, Candyman?'

Nothing.

'Breaker, Breaker to Candyman. Strummer Boy calling. You got your ears on?'

'Ten-four, Strummer Boy. What's your twenty?'

'Your gaf. Put the hammer down. I've got plans tonight.'

'Yeah alright, on my way. All good, Strummer Boy?'

'Yep, all good.'

It was pitch-black by the time Candyman arrived. As the diver handed over the package by the back door, his curiousness got the better of him. 'So what's in there, then?'

'The usual. Just hash.'

'You sure? There's a couple of metal cylinders in there too. You can feel them here, lo—'

He moved for the package and Candyman yanked it towards himself, away from the diver's reach. 'Hands off, alright? I pay you just to deliver, you nosey fuck.'

The diver stepped back cautiously, palms raised. 'No worries. Sorry.'

'Here, this is yours.' Candyman handed the diver an envelope.

He opened it, counted the cash and smiled.

'A bit extra for the extra weight. Must have been a hell of a fuckin' strain pulling that up from the seabed.'

'Aye. Too right it was. But no real bother, boss.'

'Good to know.'

As the diver tucked the envelope into his back pocket, he was sure he heard a muffled voice calling out from deep inside the house. More of a wail, but he couldn't make out the words. 'What's that noise?' he said, without thinking.

'What noise? I can't hear nothing.'

'That voice. I'm sure I just heard a voice.'

'You been chewing on that hash bar or what? There's no fucker here apart from me.'

The distant but definite wail repeated, its echo running all the way out to the back door where they stood. Their eyes locked. The diver felt a snarl in Candyman's eyes as he lowered his head and deepened his stare into the black night.

'Believe me, pal, it's nothing.'

The tension soared. The diver turned for the car, searching for words to erase the moment. 'Ah, it's just the wind moaning through that old fucking barn door there.' He chuckled falsely and shook his head. 'I must be coming down with the bends.'

'Aye. Or you will be. Now fuck off and I'll be in touch again in a couple of days. It's fog season, which means delivery season. I've got a couple more drops lined up this week, so keep that fucking tank full of air, yeah?'

'Aye, aye, boss.'

The diver left.

Candyman went to the kitchen and made a ham sandwich and a cup of tea with two sugars. He put them on a tray, added a bag of plain crisps and a biscuit from the larder and unlocked the door that led down to the basement. The man stared blankly at Candyman as he entered and put the tray on the table in front of him.

'Here you go. Supper.' He pointed at the tray. The man followed the path of the finger and picked up the Wagon Wheel.

'Eat the sandwich first. Jesus.'

The man looked afraid. His clammy hands held each other to stop them trembling.

'I'm off out now for a bit, so I'm locking the door, OK?'

'OK,' said the man.

'I'll be back before you know it, so no funny business, you got it?'

The man nodded.

Candyman turned and made his way back up the stairs, locked the cellar door, picked up the package and went out to the shed.

He switched on the old lamp that was clamped to the side of the tool bench and began to cut through the thick plastic wrapping of the package with a sharp knife. Inside was a meticulous bale of red-seal hashish. Twenty kilograms. Rich and sticky, just like the blocks of molasses he used to put in the fields for the cows to lick. He prodded it gently. It felt squidgy and smelled delicious.

Taped to the bottom end were the two metal cylinders, like giant cigar cases, covered and sealed. He took the blade, carefully cut the plastic away and popped open the tops. His heart thumped in his head as he lowered his index and middle fingers into the first tube and tugged on the bag inside. Out came the first moneybag, rattling with white tablets. He shook the cylinder and four more bags dropped out. Ten bags in all, a hundred tablets in each. He opened a bag and studied a pill, rolling it softly between his cracked thumb and weathered forefinger. It was round and thick, white with fine brown speckles. Embossed on one side was the image of a dove, the backside a splitting crease. He licked the pill with the tip of his tongue. After a moment his left eye winced from the bitterness of the chemicals and he smiled. That was the taste. He swiped his tongue across his lips to dilute the burning of the drug.

As he went to bin the cylinders, he felt a weight still inside one of them. He banged it against the workbench. A last bag dropped out, smaller, with 'Samples' scribbled on it. Inside were twenty, maybe thirty pills. Blue. He took one out and studied it. The logo of Batman was embossed meticulously on it. He'd never seen a Batman before. He huffed with amusement.

He walked over to the pile of chopped logs in the far corner of the shed, leaned over them and began to scoop them back between his legs with his right hand. They thudded and rolled on the dusty stone floor until a big old wooden box was exposed. He opened the box and placed the drugs inside, closed the lid and rebuilt the pile until the box disappeared. He dusted his hands off quickly against each other then jumped into the car and sped off along the coast road towards the Mariners.

As Mr Price leafed through the business plan, Mostyn noticed him grinding his teeth and then puffing his cheeks. He changed position with every turn of the page and began to rub his forehead with both hands.

'Who the hell wrote this for you, Mostyn?' asked Mr Price.

'Well, I dictated most of it to Paul – John from the Co-op's eldest. He's doing a business degree in the college, and he offered to help me.'

'A business degree? Really?' quizzed Mr Price sarcastically. 'I just don't get it, Mostyn. Under projected income for the next twelve months, it says here you're going to pull in fifty-six thousand pounds from the sale of one hundred and twenty cattle.'

'That's correct, Mr Price.'

'How many cattle do you have today, Mostyn?'

'About fifty-seven.'

'OK. And where are the other sixty-three going to come from?'

'Mostly young store cattle, from the mart. Sell them within twelve months then. Ready for fattening.'

'I see. And how will you pay for these sixty-three cattle, Mostyn?'

'Well, hopefully from the sale of the ones I have now, and, I was hoping, with a bit of help from the bank, Mr Price.'

'Mostyn, the sale of your current fifty-seven cattle won't make much of a dent in the loan for the cubicles and your long-overdue overdraft repayments. I see you're now nearly eleven months behind and interest on those is accruing at an alarming rate. There's not a hope in hell you are going to be able to buy any more cattle in your current circumstances.' Mr Price snapped the business plan shut and dropped it on the table. 'Mostyn, listen to me. I'm sorry, but we just cannot give you any more finance. Your outgoings have outweighed your income for some time now, and we just haven't seen you respond appropriately to your situation. You seem to carry on as normal, oblivious. The milk cheques are long gone, Mostyn. Your debt levels have been in excess of your assets for well over a year now and the deterioration over the past few months is, quite frankly, out of contr...'

A desperate haze filled Mostyn's head, blocking Mr Price's voice somewhere between his ears and his brain. He squeezed his eyes closed, then looked up. Mr Price's words came pouring back.

'...to appoint a liquidator. We have no option, as your sole creditor, than to demand the sale of the farm. If a good sale price is achieved, we could maybe discuss you keeping your harvesting machinery and possibly look to support you as a farm contractor in the local area.'

Mostyn's eyes blazed.

'I know this is a lot to take on board, Mostyn, but I'm very sorry, you are unable to sustain yourself any longer.'

Mostyn's head dropped into his hands. He closed his eyes again to frame after frame of broken images:

He's a teenager, lying at the feet of his father with his baby brother, Gareth, both wrapped in a woollen blanket, cuddling, keeping each other warm. They're on the trap coming home from their monthly trip to visit their cousins, always under the full moon; he's gazing up at the stars as the horses rock them gently along the lane, dreaming of all the things he wants to do with his young life. He's with Blodge and Huw, it's summer, just a few years later, kicking the loose straw from the trailer after unloading the stack in the big shed. The heat of the day has passed, the fresh tickle of dusk gives them new energy. They're laughing, dripping in sweat, itching with dust and pouring the cider into their tin mugs, emptying them down their thirsty necks. There was no better feeling than that. Then he's alone, in the milking parlour, just weeks before the sale of the herd. An Atlantic front looms above, rain hammering down on the tin roof. The rain falls sideways, heaved on by the force of the wind. The concrete farmyard outside swills with a torrent of dirty water and the dank and dimly-lit parlour is filled with steam from the warm sopping wet cows that troop through for milking. He pined to go back. 'What was I doing selling those cows?' He kept his face in his hands. 'Why? Why? You bloody idiot!'

Thoughts of the future hit Mostyn like a brick – sell the animals, join the queue, posh bastards take the farm, the walk to the family pew, the waster that wiped a century of graft and heritage put in place by his ancestors, who sat in the same pew with pride for a lifetime. The shame! Then dying alone in a tiny pebble-dash box in town.

He raised his head and attempted to gather himself in front of Mr Price. He could not give up. 'Are there really no other options, Mr Price? Please, there must be. You can't ask me to sell Lewis Mill. I was born in that house. Please, Mr Price. I could sell some machinery – my tractors and harvester – and just borrow Billy's from next door. That shouldn't be a problem.'

'Mostyn, try and calm yourself, please. It's all very well selling machinery, but the fact remains that your costs exceed your income, every month. Which means every month you slide deeper into debt. I know this is not fully your fault, Mostyn. The new market demands bigger farms, economies of scale, and none of us foresaw BSE. But Head Office in Cardiff has flagged your situation to me. And as the manager of the bank, I am duty bound to protect the bank's investment, and, of course, my own job. I'm sorry, Mostyn, but it really is out of my hands.' Mr Price paused to allow the information to sink in. 'Your next payments for the loan and overdraft are due on the tenth of September. It's a lot of money and it's still only a fraction of what's overdue. I could extend the liquidation decision until then if you tell me you think you could somehow meet it. But if that deadline is not met, the farm will be immediately handed over to the receivers, no question.'

Mostyn leaned forward. 'How much are those instalments, Mr Price?'

'Let me have a look.' Mr Price paused, his fingers scurrying over his calculator like a greedy mouse. 'With interest, the total comes to twenty thousand and ninety pounds.'

'Holy shit.' Mostyn sank back into the chair and stared at the ceiling above Mr Price's head. Weird Head's ugly face popped into his mind like an apparition. 'I'll make the payment, Mr Price, you can be sure of that,' said Mostyn, with as much conviction as he could muster.

'Alright then, I'll take your word for it, Mostyn. I hope you do, but take your time, it's a big decision. Think about the long term now, OK?'

'Aye, Mr Price, I will. Thank you.'

As Mostyn left the room, Mr Price lit a cigarette, picked up his phone and began to dial.

Weird Head arrived at the cave with the money in a navy sports bag around teatime on Wednesday. The tide was on its way in, so the exchange was swift and cordial. Mostyn had counted the money three times before he went to bed. He had never seen so much cash. He hid the bag in a half-empty potato sack in the larder.

As he tucked himself up in bed, Mostyn felt the tension in his body slowly release. First thing tomorrow he would go straight to pay the feed bills. That would be a good start.

A cold draught greeted Mostyn as he sauntered down the stairs for breakfast. As he entered the kitchen, he panicked. The money. The window above the kitchen table was wide open, with two smudged, muddy footprints, one on the edge of the table and one on the sill. He checked the potato sack – no bag. He scanned the kitchen, then all the rooms downstairs. The bag was gone. He grabbed his hair with both hands and clenched his fists. His eyes swept around. 'It's gone! Fucking gone!' He fell into his mouldy brown armchair, frantically rubbing his scalp. It must have been Weird Head. No one else knew. Maybe

Shifty. Maybe someone followed Weird Head. Maybe the Growler, or one of his men. It didn't really matter – the money was gone and Mostyn owed the Growler and the bank twenty grand each, both due for payment in thirty days.

Mostyn had been stoic throughout his life. He didn't really have a choice. He'd been drawn to a solitary life of responsibility and pragmatism from an early age, losing his young brother in a freak farm accident and then both his parents in quick succession in his late teens. The burden of the farm after his father's death meant he had to grow up quickly, and alone. He was accountable only to himself and every job that needed doing on the farm was his. He could not afford staff, worked day in, day out. For fifty years, he had held this faultlessly consistent demeanour, but on this summer morning, it all finally fell apart. Mr Price was right – he was finished. He would have to sell the farm, there was no other option, but he knew he would rather be dead than be driven out.

Mostyn had sunk four pints of bitter top by the time Weird Head arrived.

'Alright, Mostyn? You're becoming a regular in here these days, old boy,' said Weird Head.

'It's gone,' said Mostyn through his gritted teeth. His body shook. 'All gone!'

'What's gone?' asked Weird Head.

'What you gave me last night.'

'Well that's not my fucking problem, Mostyn. You should look after your valuables at all times. There are some bad people out there.'

'I'm very sorry to say this, but no one else knew about i—'

Weird Head grabbed Mostyn by the collar and dragged him outside, past the toilets and into the beer garden. Only Chris the landlord and deaf Colin were at the bar, and neither flinched. Weird Head pinned Mostyn up against the back wall.

'You listen to me. I didn't steal your money, you fucking shitkicker, and if you ever go there again I'll put your head in a vice and crush it like a fucking walnut, you understand me?'

'Yeah, yes, I understand. I'm sorry.'

Weird Head released him and stepped back. He looked down and saw Mostyn's trousers were soaked on one side. Weird Head laughed. 'You pathetic little man. How old are you? Still wetting your pants? Fuck me.' Weird Head smirked. 'I suggest you start repayments soon. Twenty per cent interest a week on twenty grand will quickly rack up, old boy.'

'Twenty per cent a week?'

'Aye, that's what we agreed.'

'That's four grand a week!'

'Aye, you're right, old boy. You're pretty fucking clever for a farmer.'

Mostyn slid down the wall to the floor and put his head in his hands.

Later that evening, Mostyn drove out of the farmyard without looking back. He felt resolute in defeat and focused calmly on the road ahead.

He parked up near the shore, left the car and the sand behind and started to climb up the coast path. He realised he'd not walked this way in probably thirty years, yet it was only five miles from his house. It was a clear night and the water was calm. A small swell lapped gently over the rocks on the beach below. Out to sea, six glimmering oil tankers waited patiently for their turn to enter the estuary. He wondered if any of the men on those tankers were as lonely as he was.

He reached the cliffs facing out to sea and looked north across to Rickets Head, just a few hundred yards away, resting like the head of a sleeping phoenix in the heart of St Brides Bay. He took a deep breath and continued along the undulating path.

He reached the base of the head, slid his sleeves up his forearms and began to climb. The scree was loose and he struggled for grip, but found a line. As he lifted his right leg over the last craggy outcrop, his left slipped. He began to slide. He caught hold of a thick weed that slowed his descent. He found his footing and continued upwards, finally hauling himself up onto the top of the crumbling headland.

Mostyn lay on his back and gazed up as he gathered his breath, then stood up, immediately felt dizzy and sat down again. Vertigo gripped him, but he pushed himself back up onto his feet and edged his way towards the northern side of the headland. He was surrounded on both sides by vertical drops into the shallow rocky ocean a hundred feet below. He looked for the best place to jump and found it – a small ravine embedded in the headland, allowing a clear drop into the soup of saltwater and granite boulders.

He thought of Gareth and of his parents looking down on him, seeing what their only surviving child had become. He was still that same little boy, only now he was alone in the world and bereft of hope. He wished his mother would whisper to him over the ocean on that warm salty breeze that everything was going to be all right, for him to go back home to the farm. But she never did. There was nothing. He was obsolete. He wondered if anyone would miss him or even care to look for his body. As he gazed down through the ravine, the magnetism of gravity hypnotised Mostyn. He was ready.

He looked across to Newgale and out to the twinkling lights above Solva, his toes jutting forwards, creeping over the cliff edge, then lowered his head and gaped into the void below. A reel of images flashed up out of it, the life he'd lived. The final still was one of the earliest he'd held on to: Gareth's fourth birthday, the four of them, the family. Just one step and they would be together again.

'Help! Help me! Please!' a voice shouted from further down the headland.

Mostyn swung his head towards it. 'Gareth?' he shouted. 'Gareth!' His eyes widened, blinking, squinting, until he could see a full human silhouette. It was a boy, a young man, waving his hands from an even more precarious place on the cliff. Mostyn froze against the lure of the sea.

'I don't want to die!' screamed the boy. Mostyn stepped back then shuffled his way down towards the cries, keeping his body hunched to the side of the receding rock face, clinging tight to the jagged granite outcrops as he went.

'You OK, son? Step back now, lean into the cliff. Grab my hand. Take my hand!' he yelled. The boy reached out his left hand and Mostyn clasped it. Their eyes met. They knew they were essential to one another in that moment, if to no one else in the world. Mostyn navigated the boy carefully back up the cliff until they reached flat ground and collapsed. The boy was shaking, hyperventilating. Under the spotlight of the bright moon Mostyn could clearly see that the young man lying on the ground beside him had shared his own plan.

They lay on their backs, still panting. This hadn't been it. But here Mostyn was, at the starting line, already limbered up for the long road ahead. No compass, no map, no script. He turned his head to the boy and saw the same look of helplessness.

The boy was still shivering. 'Here, wrap this around you, son.' They both sat up. Mostyn took off his coat and placed it gently around the boy's shoulders.

'What's your name, son?'

'Jethro.'

'I'm Mostyn. Thank you for saving me, Jethro.' The boy turned shyly to look at Mostyn and responded with a small reluctant smile.

They sat staring out to sea, consumed.

Jethro broke the silence. 'Why, Mostyn?'

Mostyn pondered the question. He felt protective of the boy, didn't want to hand on his own distress. He began to explain.

Jethro listened intently to Mostyn, nodding, seeming to understand.

'And you, young man. What on earth brings you to this point so early in your life?'

'Same as you, I suppose. No hope. Depression. A drug habit and a big debt to a dealer. Big debt for me at least.'

Mostyn frowned at the confession. He had always despised people who took drugs. Wasters and troublemakers.

'And I lost my dad a few months back,' continued Jethro. 'I'm just sad, Mostyn, I don't see any future for me.' His lip began to tremble.

'Now, now, son. You're only a youngster, you can't say that. Where are you from?'

'Neyland.'

'Ah, Neyland.' Mostyn smiled. 'I used to spend some time down there as a kid on the farms around Llanstadwell, with my father's friend Dai Phillips. Then, years later, we'd go down there drinking with the young farmers. We'd always get served in the Coburg when we were fifteen, sixteen. It's a bit run-down now, but it's still a special place, Neyland.'

'Yeah, special needs,' said Jethro.

'No, no. There's a community there you don't really see anymore, Jethro, but I can't really explain it. I've seen men hit seven bells out of each other and still end up singing arm in arm at the end of the night. And not just once. The spirit of togetherness there runs deep. A bit like a tribe.'

'Well, the rugby team is called the All Blacks. Same fern too,' said Jethro.

'Aye, you're right. Like a Mauri tribe,' said Mostyn.

'Yeah, they should create a Haka with a chow mein in one hand and a pint of Stella in the other.'

They both laughed.

'What's chow mein?' asked Mostyn.

'Slimy Chinese noodles.'

'*Ucha fi*,' said Mostyn, wincing. 'So who was your father? I probably knew, or at least heard of him.'

'Trevor. Trevor Jones.'

'Trevor the Brush?'

'Yep.'

'Shit. Never. Oh, Jethro, I knew your father well. I'd not seen him in the past say ten or twelve years, but he was one of the boys who was always on the harvest with us out the back of Llanstadwell. I'm going back, oof, must have been late forties I should think. I was a teenager. I think your dad was a bit younger than me. I'll never forget him flinging those bales of straw around the trailer. Dew, dew, he was a strong boy.'

'He was. And the best dad.'

'Aye, I'm sure he was. I read about his passing in the *Telegraph*, but I saw it too late to attend the funeral. I would have liked to have gone. We shared some lovely times, building up those straw loads on the banks of the estuary. They crossed my mind just now when I was standing over there looking down at the sea.'

Jethro smiled and his imagination danced. 'So what's your plan now, Mostyn?'

'Well, if I can get off this bloody headland in one piece it would be a good start.'

Jethro chuckled. 'No, seriously, what are you going to do about your farm?'

'I have to sell the lot, Jethro. I'm saddled with debts to the bank and to a moneylender who will probably cut my balls off in the next few weeks if I don't pay him.'

'Shit, that sounds heavy.'

'Aye, heavy, you could say that. And you, nipper?' asked Mostyn.

'Christ, I don't know. I'm a failure at everything. I've messed up my exams and now I'm just DJing in a few shitty clubs around the county for peanuts. I suppose I should really go back to school.'

'Yes, good plan, Jethro. Get a good education behind you, and you will always have that then. I don't even have an O level to my name, so I dread what I'm going to do for the rest of my life, if I'm honest.'

Jethro didn't respond. Something came over him. He frowned at Mostyn, and his mouth began twitching from side to side. His eyes narrowed. Mostyn didn't know what to say or do.

'How much debt do you have, Mostyn, if you don't mind me asking?'

'Urgent debt to be paid is twenty grand to the bank and twenty grand to a moneylender.'

'Where's your farm?'

'Lewis Mill, just outside Little Emlyn, smack bang in the middle of Plumstone Rock and Lion Rock, Treffgarne. Why?'

'How would you like to make enough money in one night's work to pay off at least half of your debt?'

'Ha! Sounds bloody brilliant, Jethro. Sign me up. Where's the catch?'

Jethro paused, his face changed. 'Have you ever heard of a rave party?'

'A rave party? A bloody *rave*? Christ, are you kidding me? I've seen those on the news and in the papers. Kids going crazy on drugs and all that weird music. Forget it. I saw a photo of a hippy drinking water out of a dirty puddle at one of these raves once. Savages. No way. I'm already a disgrace in the community. Having a bloody rave party will be the final nail in my coffin. No bloody way.'

'OK, OK, no problem. Chill out. Raves are cropping up all over the place and they're making a killing. Just about the entire youth of Pembrokeshire are ravers, and they're all normal kids, just like me.'

Mostyn raised his eyebrows.

'We could easily charge a tenner a head, and I reckon we could get close to a thousand punters turning up.'

'A thousand drug-fuelled lunatics on my land? Are you out of your mind, boy? No bloody chance!'

And that was the end of that.

As they navigated themselves back down off the headland, Mostyn was uneasy – the few village boys who took drugs back in the sixties and seventies were dishonest and ended up stealing or disrupting the community in some way.

Mostyn drove Jethro all the way back to Neyland, but they hardly shared a word during the thirty-minute journey. Jethro wrote his number on a Rizla paper.

'Here, Mostyn, give me a call sometime. Forget what I said about the rave. Stupid idea. I'd love to keep in touch. You saved my life tonight too. Thank you.'

Part II
Chapter 4

Mostyn's phone began to ring every hour through the night. Just two rings each time. He kept his shotgun next to his bed and barricaded all his doors with dining chairs jammed under the handles. He was sleepless. He stared at the ceiling, his body taut, his fists clenched, gripping his blankets tightly under his chin. He'd never felt so afraid and alone.

Periodically, his trembling hand reached down and held the barrel of the 12-bore. There was still one way out.

Less than a week after the night on the cliff, Mostyn noticed that one of his finest Welsh Blacks was behaving strangely. He looked wobbly, almost drunk. He had spotted something a few weeks back but turned a blind eye and prayed. But the animal was now clearly unwell. He called the vet and feared the worst. The results came back positive. The beast had BSE.

Mostyn kept him safe in a pen in the cubicle shed on fresh straw until the vet was due to arrive in the morning to put him down. He spent most of the night with the bullock, leaning up against the dirty gate, talking to him, trying to comfort him in his distress. Mostyn remembered the day he saw him for the first time. A devil of a calf. Wild as a March hare, but striking in his beauty and stature. As he grew, he calmed, his skin shone and his muscles rippled like a beast from mythology. His head was thick and perfect, sitting gracefully on those giant shoulders like a work of art, with tight black hair curls above his big, deep, lazy eyes. But those eyes were given over to confusion, lunacy and terror as it battled the vicious disease steadily breaking down its brain.

At 9.32am the bolt was fired and the beast dropped. Before the vet opened up its throat, Mostyn stepped over and kissed the thick mat of black curls and walked away. He regretted looking back and seeing the fountain of blood now gushing out of its neck and those colossal legs in their last twitches. He sobbed. He didn't know what to do or where to go; all he knew was that he didn't want to live anymore. He headed for the back lane down to the Cleddau.

'Mr Thomas,' yelled a tiny voice.

Mostyn spun around and there was young Ted, from Mill House next door, at the entrance to the lane. 'Hello, Ted,' said Mostyn, struggling to steady his voice. 'What are you doing here, son?'

'Daddy said the conkers are starting to fall, so I'm trying to find the best ones before school starts. Daddy said you have the best conker trees in this lane.'

'Did he now? Well he's right, but don't tell any other children now, will you?'

'Of course not. I'm not stupid, Mr Thomas.'

A small smile flashed across Mostyn's lips.

'Why are you crying, Mr Thomas?'

Mostyn reared back. 'Oh, Ted, one of my cattle has just gone up to heaven and I'm sad I won't see him again until I go.'

The six-year-old frowned. 'When will you go to heaven, Mr Thomas?'

'I don't know, Ted. That's up to God, not me.'

'Well, I hope you don't die soon.'

'That's very nice of you, Ted,' said Mostyn. 'Why is that then?' he probed, kindly and curiously.

'Because Mummy and Daddy said that they want you to teach me to fish for sewin and shoot rabbits. They said you need a new friend because your friend just went to heaven.'

'Did they now,' said Mostyn.

'I'd like to be your new friend, Mr Thomas, if you don't mind. I'm very brave and strong. Look.' Ted pulled back his T-shirt sleeve with his left arm, raised his right arm and tensed his tiny, wiry bicep. His body shook and his face went red as he turned to stare up expectantly at Mostyn.

Mostyn could only smile as he opened his arms wide. He went down on his knees in the dank stony lane and gave Ted a gentle hug. 'Those muscles are massive, Ted, but that's not important. Being kind, like you are now, that's what really counts. Of course you can be my new friend.'

Jethro had just pulled on his daps and was about to leave the house for chips when the phone rang.

'Hiya, boy. It's Mostyn.'

'Hey.' Jethro was startled into silence.

'Can you meet me later today? You need to tell me more about this rave thing.'

As the diver took the key from under the breeze block, his heart quickened. The wailing voice he'd heard that night from inside Candyman's house would not leave him. He had to find out.

He entered timidly through the back door and stood silently, listening, but there was nothing. He crept from room to room and found no signs of life.

Then, a faint clicking sound. He paused. It seemed to be coming from under the floorboards. He noticed an odd wooden door in the hallway, unusually narrow, and flipped the latch noiselessly to open it. An ancient stone staircase led down into the darkness, to where the noise echoed. He descended slowly and reached another door, squinting as his eyes adjusted. Two thick bolts held the door in place. The noise was very close, just behind it.

The diver opened his flick knife and pulled the doorknob towards him, quietly sliding one bolt and then the other back over the door, releasing them from the wall. He ground the doorknob slowly to the right and the door was freed. Edging it open, his keen left eye peered through the sliver of artificial light that came from the room. He opened the door further and into view came an old man, sitting on a rusted chair, facing a wall with his back to the diver, repeatedly flicking the safety flap on an electric plug socket. The old man was wearing a grey pair of polyester trousers and a burgundy V-neck sweater over a beige shirt. He was covered in stains and there were holes in the elbows of the sweater. He was thin and the top of his head was bald, but there were unkempt grey clumps of hair above both ears.

The diver froze.

The man was unaware he had company.

'Hello,' said the diver, calmly.

The old man raised his head, paused, and slowly twisted to look behind him at the diver. He frowned. 'Have you come to take me away?'

'Erm, no, no, not at all,' stuttered the diver.

'I didn't mean to do it, you know,' said the old man.

'Do what?' the diver quizzed reluctantly.

The old man paused and frowned again. 'I don't know.' His eyes glazed over and he stared at the wall to the right of the diver. Moments later, he snapped back into the diver's company. 'How long have you been my son?' asked the old man.

The diver smirked nervously. 'I'm not your son.'

'How long have you been here?' demanded the man.

'I only came in just now, to see if you're alright.'

'1927!' the old man quipped in apparent joy. He slapped his hands down hard on his knees. 'That's funny, that's the same year we won the cup.'

'What cup?'

'The FA Cup! Dew, that was some day.' The old man beamed, deep in the memory. His eyes looked up at the diver excitedly. 'St George's Day as well. Ha. We stuck it to those English bastards. Stupid bloody keeper. Dropped the ball!' He laughed.

The diver could see the man was severely affected by dementia, locked away down here in his secret little world. Yet he could not understand why Candyman kept him here. It must be his father. He considered what the old man had said and wondered if he had done something terrible. Whatever, it was not his problem. He took a biscuit from a packet on the old man's table, opened it and handed it to the man.

The old man smiled and accepted it.

'Right, I'm off now. Thank you, nice to meet you,' said the diver, edging towards the door.

'Who are you, then?' the old man asked, as if he'd set eyes on him for the first time just that second.

'Just an old friend.'

The old man huffed and smiled. His eyes glazed over again and he slowly turned back to face the wall.

The diver was halfway up the staircase when the clicking noise returned.

At 10.55pm, Mostyn and Jethro walked into the Fat Badger. Sitting at the right side of the bar was Chicken George, the local painter and decorator. He was short, tubby, with faint echoes of a rugby player's gnarled shoulders. His face was cute – a button nose splattered with freckles, set over a small mouth with plump lips. His spilling mop of curly red hair kept him looking youthful, despite being in his mid-forties. George was as daft as a brush, with the ability to trigger a tsunami of irresponsible laughter through the bar at any given moment with his idiocy.

Chicken George couldn't swim. He was terrified of water, despite growing up on the coast. The fear came from being sent away to boarding school after he failed his eleven-plus. Every night, the mistresses would dunk each boy in the stinking creamy-brown water of the tin bath and scrub them like dogs. They were dunked twice – once on arrival, then just before they were heaved out to make way for the next shivering naked boy. Water would always force its way into George's nostrils during each dunk, and he'd often think he was drowning. The sharp, uncomfortable ache that followed and the rancid smell that lingered instilled a lifetime of fear of water.

George was not the only local in the Fat Badger, or indeed the Little Emlyn parish, who could not swim. Tom and Jim Bevan, two farming brothers from the Havens, were proud they could only swim 'to the bottom'. This pride left little room for public humiliation. With George it was different, and the pub locals relished in it. Heated debates involving George would, more often than not, end with, 'Well, at least I can fucking swim, Georgie.' The pub would erupt with laughter, and the humiliation would be complete. George was the easiest bait in the Fat Badger, which gave him a misplaced sense of being unloved and unliked.

On the left side of the bar sat John the Ghost. It went without saying that John was elusive. A tall, wiry man of Russian ancestry, mid-fifties, with long blond hair, pronounced cheekbones and the purposeful facial expressions of a deep-thinking man, particularly after six pints. He'd stroll into the pub, typically in the first weeks of April, as soon as spring was in full bloom, having spent the winter 'away'. No one in Little Emlyn really knew where John would disappear to, but there was no shortage of theories. The widest-held belief was that he went to Thailand each winter to see his old lover, Wishy Squishy. He had met Wishy back in the mid-1980s in a Cardiff nightclub and had brought her back to the Fat Badger, where she inherited her surname, on several occasions to show her the sights of the county. However, things went horribly wrong when Chicken George was found behind the generator with his fingers in Wishy's pants on the night of the Young Farmers' Club tug-of-war across the river. John knocked George out cold that night, and their relationship had been frosty ever since.

The second theory was that John went to the Costa del Sol to work as a hitman in the dark months for a cockney mobster. He would never kill people, so the story went, only kneecap them. It was certainly plausible; John was a crack shot with a rifle. Farmers would hire him to shoot pigeons in their cowsheds in summer, as he was the only local marksman guaranteed not to miss and put cracks in their asbestos roofs.

Whatever the truth was, nobody really knew. When asked on his first night back in the Fat Badger where he'd been all winter, John's West Country lilt was constant each year: 'Everywhere and nowhere, boy.' His wild cackle would explode while he rolled up the sleeves of his signature red lumberjack shirt and enthusiastically deflected the conversation to enquire about the prospects for the coming harvest.

John the Ghost loved driving tractors. To spend the summers tearing around the coastal lanes and the rich patchwork of countryside between the ocean and the Preseli Hills was his idea of paradise.

Frankie Hancock always sat between Chicken George and John

the Ghost, just in case old wounds were accidentally reopened in the small hours. Frankie was a farm worker, hard as nails. Born and bred in Little Emlyn, but he was never really trusted locally as he lived in a council house and never went to chapel, even at Christmas. At sixty-two years old, he'd still never been beaten in an arm wrestle. He stood at only five foot four, but his hands were like battered shovels, his chest like a barrel. His left eye tended to head seaward after a few pints, which meant, if you didn't know to always engage his right eye, you were in for an uncomfortable interchange.

Frankie was intense. His dangerously-high blood pressure made his face burn red, like he was flat-out tamping mad, and his eyes looked ready to burst into tears at any moment.

Lastly, sat at the left side of the bar, was the new addition, Boutros. Boutros had recently retired to Pembrokeshire after a career in the United Nations. He'd been coming to the Welsh coast ever since he was a child, on summer holidays with his parents. He continued the tradition, though much less religiously, with his own children, and vowed to retire one day to one of the villages on the coast between Broad Haven and Newgale.

His wife, Dolly, passed away with cancer in the year of their retirement, only six months after arriving in their dream home overlooking Nolton Haven.

Boutros fell into a deep depression until a chance meeting with Frankie the previous autumn. Frankie scolded Boutros when he spotted him stealing blackberries from Jim Bevan's lane. After a mild kerfuffle, Frankie sensed the sadness in him and backed off, but he was intrigued by this eccentrically dressed man and his very posh accent. They got talking. When Frankie heard about the passing of Boutros's wife, he welled up and confessed to Boutros how awful he was to his own wife, Betty.

Betty had looked after Frankie immaculately, ever since they wed at the age of seventeen. But time and gravity had not been kind to Betty, and Frankie had become embarrassed by her. 'A face like a melted welly' was how he often described Betty, which was why he claimed to spend so much time down the Fat Badger.

Upon confession, Boutros told him straight, right there in the lane, that he should stop that behaviour immediately. Frankie agreed as tears rolled down his face. They embraced and one of the most unlikely friendships was born.

Boutros, whose real name was Nigel Green, was introduced to the Fat Badger a few days later. Surprisingly, he'd never been there, not even for a pint, in all his years of visiting, as Little Emlyn was tucked secretly away, five miles from the coast, through the rabbit warren of lanes that led inland. Within two days, after hearing tales of his years in Arabia and the Far East, the boys at the Fat Badger were mesmerised, and Nigel was renamed Boutros.

Jules Gent was the owner of the Fat Badger. He was not your typical Pembrokeshire landlord. Firstly, he was gay. Out and proud. He'd bought the pub with his savings, having worked for years through the eighties in London as a sound engineer on popular prime-time TV shows. Jules had purportedly slept with a host of big-name gay celebrities and claimed to be the first person to have embraced Freddie Mercury offstage after *that* Live Aid performance.

Secondly, he disliked people. Especially families – the same ones every year that poured into the pub. Dads acting like locals, claiming to be Jules's close friends. He despised them all, except for the odd bi-curious father, who was as rare as a hen's tooth in Little Emlyn. Children, they just tore the cloth of the pool table, squished their chips into the red paisley carpet and defaced his magnolia walls with ketchup fingerprints. Mothers, females, they never stood a chance, especially the drinkers. In Jules's eyes they'd shuffle up to the bar, guts bulging, wobbling through their hoisted leggings like giant cysts.

Jules only had one true friend in the world – Duncan, his ageing pug. Duncan was twelve years old and was not in good shape. Within a month of moving into the pub, six years previously, Duncan had stopped eating conventional dog food. He had developed an insatiable appetite for burgers and chips, being fed all the scraps by punters and staff. As much as Jules tried to stop it, he could not reverse Duncan's voracious obsession. He tried everything, but in the end the only workable solution was to stuff vitamins and minerals into Duncan's burgers and to sprinkle them with revolutionary bacteria and plant powders like spirulina and wheatgrass, recommended to him by Vince the Mince, his former lover, a nutritionist at a cutting-edge health club in Soho. Duncan even had his own fridge in the pub kitchen – half-full of cold burgers and half-full of multicoloured pills and green powders.

Despite Jules's expensive attempt to keep Duncan healthy, the old dog's hind legs had packed in a few months back, after a busy and gluttonous bank holiday Easter weekend. He was unable to sustain the weight of his swollen stomach any longer. He often sat quite happily in his own faeces, and Jules began to wonder if the time would soon come for him to have to make the Big Decision. But it was tough – Duncan had been there for him through all of the hard times. Losing friend after friend to AIDS. Watching old lovers wither in agony down to skin and bone. The abuse, the stigma he faced as the virus spread through the city, reinforcing the prejudices and discrimination against a perceived vermin underclass of gay men romping like brainless baboons in the sweaty dance pits of old London Town.

Duncan was always there for him, his rock, when the whole world seemed to be against him and his loved ones steadily decayed.

By 1988, Jules had had enough. He had to get out. He was still clean. Remarkably. And he could no longer tolerate being spat at every time he left Heaven in the early hours of Sunday mornings, frowned upon like a leper as he walked the streets with his friends. By the end of August, Jules had purchased the Fat Badger, moved himself and Duncan to Pembrokeshire, and Little Emlyn would never be the same again.

'You can fuck off, Mostyn. You tight fucking farmers, drinking at home, then coming in here for last orders expecting a lock-in. You do my fucking head in,' squeaked Jules.

'Sorry, Jules. I've had a busy night trying to get the baler started, and I promised to meet young Jethro here for a pint. We'll just have the one, I promise.'

'Yeah, yeah, just the one. How many times have I heard that, you sexy bastard,' said Jules, pulling down Mostyn's tankard and pumping it full of ale.

'Nice to meet you, Jethro. What you doing with this old fart?' asked Jules. 'I hope he's shaved his arse, back and crack for you, love. He never did for me.'

Mostyn smiled at Jules and shook his head with affectionate disbelief. Jethro didn't know where to look and forced a smile as he pulled the hood down off the back of his head.

'Hi,' he said.

'I'm only messing, love. What can I get you?'

'Pint of lager, please.'

They sat down under the stuffed badgers and began to talk.

'So what happens if the police find out?' began Mostyn, picking up from his inquisition on the walk down to the pub.

'They won't. If this field's where you say it is, how the hell are they going to hear it from town? And if they do, they'll never find their way down there.'

'Maybe one of the neighbours will call the police.'

'You said you had one posh guy next door who was alright. Maybe you should let him know, but just say it's a young farmers' barbecue and disco. Don't mention the word rave.'

'Aye, I'm not fucking stupid, son.'

'So you can take me down to the field in the morning, yeah?'

'Aye.'

As the last tourists filtered out of the pub, only George, Frankie, John and Boutros remained at the bar, while Mostyn and Jethro continued in whispers across the floor. Jules locked the door, drew the curtains and dimmed the lights.

'Are you sure these guys are alright?' asked Jethro nervously.

'Aye, son. They don't look very dynamic, I know. But there's a lot of experience and skills sitting at that bar.'

They stood up from their chairs and meandered over to the empty side of the L-shaped bar.

It took several minutes for Frankie to pause from his rant about the fading quality of baler twine and down the half pint he had neglected during the tirade. Mostyn pounced as the last spittle of froth slid into Frankie's mouth.

'So, boys. Me and young Jethro here would like to ask you all for some help.'

All five of them fell silent, put down their glasses and turned their heads to look at Mostyn. Very rarely were they called on for assistance, and never collectively.

'Really?' asked Chicken George.

'Aye,' said Mostyn.

'You must be fuckin' desperate,' said Jules, disappearing into the kitchen.

'We're all ears, Most,' said John the Ghost.

'Well, as you probably know, I've been in a spot of financial trouble lately due to all the shit that's going on with this bloody common market and BSE. And it's got pretty bad lately with the bank, and I need to do something pretty urgently to help me out of my rut.'

'Aye, I hear you, Most,' said Frankie. 'What you boys are going through now is shocking. I've not seen it so bad in all my years farming.'

The rest of the bar nodded respectfully.

'Well, young Jethro here has come up with a plan. It's probably going to sound a bit crazy.'

'A knocking shop in town?' chipped in Chicken George.

John the Ghost rolled his eyes.

'No, George,' said Mostyn. He paused for a moment, his eyes springing from man to man. 'A rave.'

There was silence for a few seconds as the two words sank in.

'A rave?' exclaimed Frankie. 'A fucking rave? Have you lost your marbles, Mostyn? The *Daily Mail* has got pictures in it every week of those kids on that ecstasy, wobbling their heads and making funny shapes with their hands to that fucking spaceman music. All hell let loose. You need your bloody head read if you do that, boy.'

'Frankie,' said Mostyn calmly, 'my farm is going to be taken away from me next month unless I do something. I'm up to my nuts in debt. If you can think of something that can get me close to twenty grand in the next two weeks, please let me know. You know that farm is my life. My great-grandfather bought it, and it's been run immaculately until recently. You know more than anyone the problems we've had. And most of them are out of our control, that's the bloody frustrating thing. And now it looks like I'm going to be turfed out. If I don't come up with something pretty damn quick, I'll be living in those housing association homes by the end of the year, spending my days in the job centre while some posh English bastard is returfing my lawn for his fucking croquet pitch. Sorry, Boutros, no offence intended.'

'Don't worry, old boy, none taken,' said Boutros solemnly.

'And who the hell is going to employ a sixty-four-year-old, uneducated, washed-up, bankrupt farmer?' continued Mostyn.

'So tell us then, Most, what can us lot do to help?' asked George.

'I'll let Jethro here fill you in on the details.'

'Fucking hell,' said Jules, 'fresh pints then, boys?'

'Aye, aye, better had,' said John, putting out his cigarette. 'This could be a long night.'

They all took a toilet break as Jules filled their glasses. They returned, rubbing their hands in anticipation and settled back onto their stools.

Jethro's drawn face came alive as he began to conjure up the dreamy scenario. 'OK, gents, on Saturday the twenty-seventh of August we have a perfect storm of parties going on down in Tenby. It's bank holiday weekend, which is the biggest weekend of the year. Chequers and the Night Owl are going head to head for the biggest club night of the year. In Chequers they've got two DJs from the Gardening Club in London, and at Up for It! in the Night Owl there's Danny Slade and Jon of the Pleased Wimmin.'

The men frowned, all staring blankly at Jethro.

'A gardening club and Jon of the pleased women?' quizzed Frankie.

'What the fuck are you talking about, boy?'

'Sorry. The Gardening Club is in Covent Garden, one of the top clubs in London. And Jon of the Pleased Wimmin is a transvestite DJ, a man dressed as a beautiful woman. He's the best party DJ out there.'

'Fucking hell, Mostyn,' continued Frankie, 'Jon of the pleased women, a transvestite DJ. Well. I've heard it all now.'

The other men stayed focused, intrigued.

'On top of that,' continued Jethro, 'the day before, the Radio One Roadshow will be in South Beach, Tenby. So in all, we've got potentially three hundred clubbers in Chequers, at least four hundred in the Night Owl, and probably a couple hundred at the Roadshow. The general plan is to spend the week before the rave flyering around Tenby, at the pubs, obviously targeting the clubbers, then at the Roadshow on the Friday. On rave night, we'll blitz Chequers and the Night Owl with floods of flyers. We'll make Canaston Bowl near Oakwood the meet-up point for cars. Everyone knows that place, it's in the middle of nowhere, and the car park is massive. We'll then split off several convoys through the country lanes, all the way back to Little Emlyn and to Lewis Mill, where we'll all be waiting to unveil the greatest rave in the history of mankind: Lewistock!'

'Lewistock!' exclaimed George. 'Tidy fucking darts! What have I been missing? Count me in, boy!'

The other men looked at each other and were clearly excited, but John dampened the mood. 'But aren't these raves illegal, Jethro?'

'Well, not really. They're trying to bring in this new Criminal Justice Act to stop them, but I'm pretty sure it's not been passed yet. And as long as you don't charge any money for admission, then it's all kosher.'

'Well that's no fucking good then, is it?!' said Frankie.

'No, but who's going to be checking if we're charging?' said Jethro. 'No one's going to find it if the site is as remote as what Mostyn says it is.'

It took only two more pints for all the boys to commit. Jethro explained the general plan and delegated all of the tasks to the team. Chicken George – head of power supply, lights and set design; John the Ghost – marquee hire, straw bales for seating, dance podiums and signposting; Frankie – doorman; Jules – the bar; and Boutros – driver for the flyer distributors. Jethro would organise the DJs, decks, the sound system and the convoys from Canaston Bowl, while Mostyn would make sure the lanes down to the site were tidy, and, of course, oversee the safety of the farm.

Excitement crackled around the pub in the wee hours of that morning. Nothing as adventurous in scale or complexity had been attempted in these parts since time began. Jethro and Mostyn left the Fat Badger feeling sure they had recruited the elite squad for the job.

As they walked into the darkness, a van approached from behind. George rolled down his window as he drew alongside them. 'Lift, boys?'

Mostyn frowned. 'What the hell you driving for? You stupid bastard.'

'Too pissed to walk, Most.'

'Nah, go on, we're tidy. You take it easy up the hill now.'

Mostyn and Jethro arrived back at Lewis Mill at around 4am to a small green shoebox waiting for them on Mostyn's front doormat. Mostyn's fingers trembled as he opened it. Inside was the severed head of a rat and a note: 'Welcome to the rat race.'

Chapter 5

'This is perfect,' said Jethro, twirling around, arms gliding, surveying the field. It was flat, with lush grass, set in a steep and thickly-wooded valley. The Cleddau flowed along its southern boundary. This isolated river valley stretched for miles both upstream and down, but Mostyn's land was one of the most remote points, being at the halfway mark between Treffgarne Bridge and the Old Bridge in town.

Jethro smiled and his mind floated. 'No one will hear us down here,' he whispered to himself.

They strolled down to the river. Jethro took in the sight and soft sound of his feet brushing through the long grass. It had been so long since he'd appreciated it. They sat in silence, looking out over the current as it meandered around the horseshoe bend.

'What do you think he meant by "Welcome to the rat race?"' asked Mostyn softly.

'I honestly don't know, Most. I think he's just trying to mess with your head.'

'Well, he's doing a bloody good job at that.'

'Look, Mostyn, you just owe the cunt twenty grand, simple as that. You just need to pay him back, rat race or no rat race, that's the deal.'

'But I'm sure it was him that stole it back from me. It had to be,' said Mostyn.

'Can you prove it?'

'Nope.'

'Well you're screwed then. Sorry, Most, but you are. You should never have got involved with him in the first place.'

'Aye, I know you're right, son. Same for you too, mind, you righteous little shit. This Ronnie sounds like bad news. When are you due to pay him back?'

'Christ, a week ago. He's been asking around after me. He's even come into Neyland looking for me. He lives somewhere up on the other side of St David's.'

'Shit, that's a journey. He's keen,' said Mostyn.

Silence returned and Mostyn studied Jethro as the boy dozed on the bank, trying to remember what he himself was like at the same age. At nineteen, he'd already been working full-time for four years, mostly with horses in the fields. He remembered Banky the shire horse, the gentle giant, and how he used to run under her belly as a kid with Skip, his springer spaniel; the fishing trips with his grandfather to this very spot, where they lay on the bend around the big pool, fly-fishing at dusk; the tranquillity of the river valley in summer, the flash of a kingfisher in flight, the early evening heat shimmering on the warm silent earth. But now he was alone, and those memories seemed almost to be someone else's – they were so distant. His only family now was this near-stranger of a boy, with as many problems as himself, from a generation he shared no common ground with, who he was about to entrust with his fate.

Mostyn had worked tirelessly to remain an upstanding member the Little Emlyn community for six decades. If the rave went horribly wrong, and he could see much room for that eventuality, he knew his whole life's effort would have been for nothing. The shame of his demise would haunt him all the way to his grave. But he had to keep faith in Jethro, and the rave. It was the only hope he had of keeping his farm, if only for a few more months, until beef prices went up or some other way to raise money arose.

'Alright, I'm after a generator,' said George.

'What for?' said the man from the plant hire shop.

'For a sound system and lighting.'

'OK. For what event is it?'

'Er...a Brawdy Young Farmers' disco. In a field.'

'Oh, are Brawdy YFC having a party? Brilliant! I live in Solva. A few of my mates are in the YFC.'

Shit, thought George. He searched for a quick lie. 'Aye, well, it's not a hundred per cent confirmed yet. They're waiting to see if they can definitely get a pig roast booked in for it.'

'A pig roast?' quizzed the man. 'Having a pig roast or not will decide if a YFC disco in a field will go ahead or not?'

'Aye,' said George, 'you know what those bloody farmers are like.'

'Can't they just get a burger van?'

'No,' said George, 'farmers don't like burgers. They don't trust the meat, probably know too much. But a big juicy piggy now, they'll fuckin' trough that down like there's no tomorrow.'

The man looked lost for words.

'So, generator?' asked George firmly, wiggling his eyebrows.

'Oh, yeah. Sorry. How big do you want it? Will it be outdoors or inside a marquee? How many people you expecting?'

'Christ, I don't know all the details. All I know is that they're expecting about a thousand, I think.'

'A thousand people for a Brawdy YFC disco in a field? Are you mental?'

'Er...they've got a big band coming down. From away.'

'A "big band"? How big?'

'Er, big, I think.' George's mind finally began to flatline. He was going to get rumbled on the first hurdle by a tool-shop geek. Everyone would find out. There would be no rave, and Mostyn would lose the farm.

'Red red wine,' blurted George, as shocked with his chosen three words as much as the man was.

'What do you mean?' said the man, frowning. 'You mean UB40 are going to come and play at a Brawdy YFC disco in a field? UB fucking 40?'

'Aye,' said George. 'Them are the ones.'

'Seriously?' asked the man. He began to believe George. Why would someone make such a story up?

'Aye, but like I said, no pig roast, no UB40. I tell you what, let me find out for sure. Once I know, I'll come back to you in the week.'

'Yes, yes, no problem,' said the man, imagining the possibilities of such an event.

Bollocks, thought George as he left the shop. 'Red red wine. Fucking idiot.'

Mostyn had just put the kettle on for his last cup of coffee before bed when he was startled by torchlight in the backyard. It was almost 11pm. Footsteps. He quickly slapped the bolt across the back door and dashed into the larder.

There was a pounding on the loose glass pane, but Mostyn didn't move. He heard Weird Head mumbling.

A black boot came through the glass, then a fist. It found the bolt and slid it back. The door handle squealed open.

'Mostyn!' shouted Weird Head. 'I've come to join you for a bedtime cuppa, old boy. I've bought a couple of friends along. Hope you don't mind.'

In walked two chubby young thugs, both not more than twenty-five. One had a legacy of acne spread over a heavily snouted face and a tattoo of the Neyland fern down the left side of his neck. The other, not as portly but equally menacing, had spiky brown hair and wore a black Megadeth T-shirt.

'Come out, come out, wherever you are,' sang Weird Head.

Mostyn couldn't take it. He walked straight out of the larder and hung his head in front of Weird Head.

'Hello, Mostyn. Lovely to see you, old boy.' Weird Head walked up to Mostyn and slapped the top of his left arm, hard. He stumbled sideways and Weird Head took a step further into his space.

'Can you fix me and the boys here a cup each of that fine Mellow Birds?'

Mostyn shuffled over to the kitchen and added more water to the kettle. His hands shook as he pondered his options. He couldn't scream for help; the nearest farm was half a mile away.

'Have you been avoiding me, Mostyn?' said Weird Head.

'No, no, of course not. I've just been busy. I've got cattle going in a few days, lots of paperwork to do.'

'Farmers do paperwork, do they, Mostyn? That surprises me.'

Mostyn was silent.

'Maybe your cattle will go tonight, old boy. No paperwork required. How does that sound?'

Mostyn was paralysed. He didn't respond.

'Are you ignoring me, you washed-up shitkicker?' Weird Head prompted the thugs to grab Mostyn. They clasped his ageing frame and slammed him up against the stone wall. 'It's been two weeks now and I've not heard a peep about repayments from you, old boy. That's eight grand, just in interest. When can I expect some cash? Or would you prefer I took some assets instead?'

The thugs tightened their grip and snarled, tilting their heads even closer towards Mostyn's face.

Weird Head looked around the kitchen. He smirked as he picked up a photo of Mostyn's parents on their wedding day, set in a gilded silver frame. He stroked his mother's image gently with the back of his thick index finger, up and down her entire body, groaning quietly as he circled the contours of her breasts.

'You stole the money from my house, you bastard,' screamed Mostyn.

A shower of blows collapsed Mostyn to the floor, blood swilling in his mouth.

'You ever heard of the Growler, old boy?' said Weird Head, unmoved, looking down at Mostyn over his mug.

'Yes,' said Mostyn.

'Good. Have you ever set eyes on him?'

'No.'

'Huh.' Weird Head grinned and stooped down until his face was inches from Mostyn's. 'Well if you think I'm big and ugly, wait till you meet the gaffer. And you will meet him one day, Mostyn, very soon, when you least hope to, if you don't pay him back the money he so kindly lent you.'

Weird Head grabbed Mostyn's bloodied chin. 'Four grand, by next Friday, or the receivers will be in, and they don't put a high value on much. Got it?'

In his haze, Mostyn tried to calculate the days to the rave. 'Give me two weeks, please, and I'll give you eight thousand. I promise.'

'You promise? That's cute, Mostyn. Yeah, OK, let's work with that. But if you fuck us about just a teeny bit, the gaffer will remove your knackers while I empty your sheds. Understood?'

'Yes, understood.'

Mostyn held his bloodied head in his hands as the torches slashed their way back up the lane.

John the Ghost was more streetwise than Chicken George. He'd travelled, been away as much as at home over his eventful life.

'Hi there. I'd like to hire a big marquee, please,' said John.

'OK. What's it for?' asked the man.

'A big rave down in Little Emlyn on bank holiday weekend, for a thousand ravers. You should come down, mate. There'll be tits and fanny everywhere.'

The man laughed nervously.

'No, only kidding. It's for a YFC do, just over the border in Cardigan, I forget which one. The young famers in my local just sent me here on a whim when they saw your offer in the paper last night.'

'Ah, OK, yes I see,' said the man. 'Yes, it's a great offer, isn't it?'

'It is,' said John.

Five minutes later, John walked out of the surplus store with a receipt for an eighty by fifty foot marquee for the bank holiday weekend and not a sniff of suspicion raised.

'We need to get all of the ravers, surfers and crusties from North Pembs down too. They're all mad for it,' said Biscuits.

'How do you know about them?' asked Jethro.

'George was telling me the other day. Go on, tell him, George.'

'Aye, aye, they fucking love it, up north. There's more wacky baccy smoked north of here than in Amsterdam and I've heard the kids are dancing all night off their heads in the rugby club in St David's. I was painting a fence for one of the deacons in the cathedral a few weeks back, and he was telling me that the entire youth up there had become possessed. He said they had all been infected with this evil ritualistic music and drugs from the devil. He said only God could save them now. Funny as fuck, it was.'

'Perfect,' said Jethro. 'So what's the best way to speak to them? Where do they all drink? We don't really know anyone up there.'

'Well, first I'd go see the surfers in Newgale. There are loads of them now, and they're all puffing away in their campervans, wobbling their heads to some fucking drug music I don't know. Go to the middle car park when there's surf and ask around for Potts. He's the big daddy, lungs of steel by all accounts. He's got a split-screen, nice mustard colour. Can't miss it.'

'Tidy,' said Jethro.

'And then there's Gurnard and his turbo painters up in St David's. First thing you should know is that you can't mix these two groups together.'

'Who? The painters and the surfers?'

'Aye. Well, Gurnard and Potts anyway.'

'Why not?'

'They say Gurnard fingered Potts's mother in the back of a taxi on the way back from town last summer, after RJ's.'

'Jesus,' said Jethro.

'Aye. Didn't go down too well.'

'Surprising,' said Biscuits.

'Hell of a boy for the women. And the beer,' said George.

'Anyway,' George continued, 'the turbo painters, they're clean off, taking that whizz, whatever that is. They only work three days a week cos they paint so fast.'

'Gurnard?' quizzed Jethro.

'Aye, that's what he goes by now. His real name's Bernard.'

'Need I ask about the transition?' asked Jethro.

'Well, it's something to do with his chin wob—'

'Aye, we know. Only messing, George.'

George looked confused but carried on. 'Yeah, well, these boys, they know everyone from Solva to St David's, all the way to Fishguard. They've painted most of the north of the county this past twelve months on that whizz. They're a riot. The farmers love them cos they charge by the hour, the shops and landlords all love them cos they're always spending, and the horsey chicks, now they fucking dig the turbo painters. Top shaggers apparently. If we get Gurnard and the boys on side, we can guarantee they'll bring twenty or thirty of those smoking hot horsey birds. Maybe even more.'

'You'd better not be lying now,' said Jethro, angling a stare at George.

'On my life, boy.'

As Janice salted his chips, Jethro could see his mother was still as empty and lost as the day they buried his dad. She had been robbed of the retirement they had worked for for over forty years, and the fact of it colonised her face. She looked to Jethro as if she had withdrawn from living, drifting around the streets of Neyland from job to job like a used-up crisp packet. So depressed was her conversation that Jethro feared if he raised his problems with her, his own mother, she would likely suggest they jump off the cliffs together.

'Thanks, Mum.'

'That's alright, son. See you later,' said Janice, her back to Jethro as he left the shop. She had done little to console him and his brother, Jac, after their father's accident. They'd grieved together, like orphans. Their father was dead, and within days, so it seemed was their mother.

Jethro heard footsteps quickening behind him as he approached the corner of his street. He slowed, and so did the footsteps. He swung his head around, bunching his shoulders through instinct. A grainy hand clasped his neck and his eyes met with Ronnie's.

'Gotcha! Ya little prick. Where the fuck have you been, big stuff?' he asked, his Scottish drawl sinister.

'I-I-I,' Jethro stuttered, 'I lost all the pills at that party. All of them. I took too many mushrooms and lost everything. I'm really, really sorry, Ronnie.' Jethro could see Ronnie's deep wrinkles under the evening shadows, his head – pale, drawn and bald – reminding Jethro of Hellraiser.

'Don't be sorry, boy, you still owe me two grand. I know it's coming.' Ronnie tightened his grip on Jethro's throat and led him into the alleyway behind his house. 'If you can't handle your drugs, pussy boy,

I suggest you stop taking them. It can be an expensive habit. Now, I know where you live, and I know your ma has a long dark walk home late at night. So let's not let anything untoward damage our relationship further until the transaction is complete. Understood?'

'Yes. Understood,' said Jethro clinically. He was surprised by his own calmness, his lack of fear, even at the hands of this mobster. Maybe he was immune, desensitised to life.

'Good, good. You get me a grand by the first of September, then the second by the fourteenth, and we're square, you little fucking runt. You got that?'

'Yes.'

'And if you fuck me about, son, I will take it out on your mother's wee arse. I know she's on her own now. I didn't realise that was your old man who fell from the bridge. Quite a story. Now let's not let more tragedy strike the Jones household, OK, my boy?'

Jethro knew something was amiss when he saw Mostyn's wellies covered in muck and lying strewn on the slabs outside the front door in the morning sun. Jethro had observed him taking his wellies off before, the way he delicately hosed them down and settled them perpendicular to the wall. He put his bike up against the garage wall and walked up to the house. The front door was open.

'Mostyn,' he called.

'Aye, come on in,' Mostyn shouted back. Jethro walked into the kitchen and found Mostyn observing a carnival of birds and squirrels fighting for control of the hanging nut cages out on the back lawn. Mostyn's silence unnerved Jethro.

'Look at those fucking squirrels. They've seen off some beautiful woodpeckers, jays and young blue tits over the past few weeks. I've just about had it. Look how fucking fat they are.'

Jethro could see this injustice consuming Mostyn as they both watched. One of the squirrels pounced on a landing blue tit. This was the last straw. Mostyn leaped out of his chair.

'Right, that's it, you little bastards.' He stomped into his office, unlocked his shotgun from its cabinet, loaded it with two cartridges and slid the barrel slowly out through the side curtain of the window, blowing the two squirrels, the nut cages and birdhouse to smithereens. He then calmly emptied the used cartridges, put the gun back in its place, locked it, walked back out to the kitchen, straight through the patio doors and up the steps up onto the lawn in his socks. He picked up the two fat sacks of blood-soaked fluff and threw them, without ceremony, over the hedge into the woods below.

'Feel better now?' asked Jethro.

'Aye,' said Mostyn, 'I do. Do you know what, son? Fuck it. Fuck it all. My mother always said to me, "Don't let the bastards get you down, son." Now I'm telling you the same. We have to get this show on the road and not worry about those fucking bullies. I can't live with this fear anymore. The worst-case scenario, if it all goes tits up, is that I sell my little piece of paradise here, clear our debts and I'll buy a little cottage in the village, and you can come look after me. How's that sound?'

Jethro already knew Mostyn well enough to be sure the only way he would be forced from the farm would be in a box. But they needed to move forward. 'Well, let's hope it won't come to that. This place is beautiful, Most. But, yeah, you've got a deal there. If it all goes tits up.'

The battered yellow Maestro van spluttered down the busy high street, its horn bleating like a dying sheep as a group of teenagers spilled off the pavement. The van swerved, missing them by inches. The telescopic ladder rattled out of the roof rack, stopping inches from the back windscreen of the car ahead. The van driver extended his right hand out of the window and scuttled it back efficiently.

The faded British Telecom decal was still visible on the van's panels, and the fingerprints of paint dotted all over the vehicle indicated that an authentic Pembrokeshire cowboy had just rolled into the city.

St David's, Britain's smallest city. A windswept outpost on the remote St David's peninsula of West Wales. An ancient settlement with a rich history and a staggeringly grand cathedral that had been visited by famous pilgrims and warriors over the centuries, from Kings Henry II to Edward I to William the Conqueror in 1077.

Chicken George stepped out of the van. A slow-motion whip of his arm removed his sunglasses. He breathed in deeply to expand his chest, floods of tourists scurrying in and out of the gift shops and cafes.

Banging came from the back of the van.

'Shit,' said George. He reached for the back doors and swung them open.

'Jesus, George, we nearly fucking suffocated in there,' said Jethro. He and Biscuits clambered over the paint pots, rollers, ladders, dirty overalls and tools to get out of the sweltering heat of the van.

'Sorry, boys, I was distracted by all the fanny. It's fuckin' lifting. Look at it.'

The boys didn't look. They had been briefed on George's taste in women by John the Ghost, which had made them shudder at the time.

'It must have been thirty-five degrees in there. I'm fucking soppin' now,' moaned Biscuits, dabbing his forehead with the sleeve of his T-shirt.

'Will you stop whinging?' said George. 'If my van isn't up to your standards, boys, you can fucking walk home tonight, you ungrateful pair of pricks.'

George leaned into the van and pulled a clean piece of ripped bed sheet from a bucket. 'Here, use this.'

The sun had begun its descent, its technicolour glow over the busy streets saturating the stone terraces. Jethro and Biscuits smiled to themselves, soaking up the mid-summer ambiance as families flocked from the beaches.

'Feel like I'm on holiday,' said Biscuits.

'Aye. I was thinking the same,' said Jethro.

They walked into the Farmer's Arms just in time for happy hour.

The turbo painters were known to down tools and be in the Farmer's in time for the 5pm happy hour on weeknights, especially in summer. They always sat at the same table in the beer garden, with full view of the back door, always on the lookout for 'tail'. They drank snakebite and black like it was going out of fashion, and the roars of laughter as they sparred jibes at each other were infectious. They rarely washed or changed out of their painting clothes until the weekend, but that didn't deter the ladies. The excessive amphetamine consumption and outdoor work gave them the fantastically misleading appearance of being extremely fit and healthy young men, and their aura was magnetic.

On the left sat Deri, a former school football captain with a washboard six-pack, the sole remaining legacy of his sporting glory. The only son in a family with four older sisters, Deri's easy charm and soft accent had the girls queuing. His demise into a turbo-painting raver saddened and disappointed his parents, his former teachers and the coaches at the football club, but he didn't care – he was eighteen, independent, a local sex god and living in the moment with his best mates.

Next to Deri sat Sparky, the loveable livewire. Small and skinny, with thick curly blond hair, a small turned-up nose and freckles. There was madness in Sparky's eyes and an intense soul that was restless and reckless. He'd grown up in a pub in Abercynon, in the Cynon Valley of south Wales, surrounded by coal miners. His father, the landlord, was turfed out by the brewery in 1987 as the business sank along with the local coal mine. At the age of twelve, Sparky relocated to St David's with his mother, Rita, who'd left his father for the fresh sea air of Pembrokeshire, and for another woman, who she'd met at a Royal Welsh Show sheepdog agility competition.

This upheaval had left Sparky lonely, angry and fearless. He was attracted by the escapism that surfing offered and grew quickly into a young surfing prodigy who, by the age of fourteen, was regularly ripping in big winter waves at the Elevator at Whitesands Bay. He entered into local surfing folklore during the final of the Pembrokeshire Open in 1990, dropping into a ten-foot bomb, backhand, at the left at Abereiddy, a gloomy black slate bay that stirred only on the biggest of winter swells. The hateful walls of water that marched in from the mid-Atlantic spooked most of the surfing community with rare but horrific sneaker sets that closed out the bay, washing up the surfers like drowned seals.

Sparky not only made the drop, but buried his rail so deep on the bottom turn that he tore back up the face of the wave as if he were being sucked up by its raw power. His fast vertical top turn sent up a torrent of spray. The crowd gasped as he re-entered the wave and flew across its colossal face as the avalanche of water tried, but failed, to catch him. He launched toward the sky as the wave closed out and the spectators went wild. He won the contest. He was only fifteen, the youngest winner in its history.

Sparky needed stimulation to cope with having a lesbian for a mother. The rugby boys at school would chant 'Rita, Rita, fanny eater' but he was helpless to retaliate, and he had no hard friends to back him up. He turned to cider and hash at sixteen and soon hooked up with Deri and Bernard. Although they had all followed very different paths through childhood and adolescence, they quickly realised their mutual love for excess. The relationship blossomed and within two years, they'd all flunked their A levels, developed a passion for amphetamines and rave music, dropped out of school and set up the turbo painters business.

Normally, Gurnard, the most accomplished waster in north Pembrokeshire, sat on the right side of the table. Useless in all aspects of work except self-promotion, Gurnard was absent tonight, likely out canvassing for more painting jobs around the coastal pubs.

Just Deri and Sparky sat there chatting quietly, smoking rollies with occasional fits of laughter. George had worked with the turbo painters on several big jobs, so they knew each other quite well.

Jethro bought the beers and they walked over.

'Alright?' said George.

'Alright, George,' said Sparky.

'Aye, tidy. Can't complain.'

'What you boys up to?'

'Fuck all really, apart from work. Busy time now. You busy?'

'Aye,' said George. 'Flat out. Got a few farmhouses down Camrose way.'

'Tidy.'

'Gurnard about?' asked George.

'Nah, he's up the country club tonight,' said Deri.

'Which one?'

'Which one? North Pembs Country Club, you minge. How many other country clubs do you know round here?'

'You mean the one Glyn Llewellyn put on his farm?'

'Aye.'

'Ah, OK. We'll head up there now in a bit. Mind if we join you for a pint?'

'Course not. Pull up a pew.'

'Tidy. Cheers,' said Jethro.

'Where you boys from then? Haverfuckfest?' said Sparky, with a smile.

'No,' said Jethro, sniggering. 'Neyland.'

'Ooof, even better.'

'You cheeky bastard,' said Biscuits.

The pints went down quickly and conversation flowed. George left them to it and went and sat at the bar. By eight o'clock, Jethro, Biscuits, Deri and Sparky were on a mission, dabbing speed under the table and sinking the snakebite at a quickening pace.

George staggered out to the beer garden just as darkness fell. 'Have you told them about Lewistock yet, Jethro?'

'Just building up to it.'

'What's Lewistock?' quizzed Sparky, his lower lip frantically massaging the top.

'Let's go into the bar. I'm fucking freezing out here,' said Jethro. 'I'll tell you in there.'

The pub was packed. The weekend had landed. All the young movers and shakers of St David's were shoulder to shoulder in the Farmer's.

'Listen to this, boys and girls,' announced Sparky as they entered the pub through the back doors. 'Jethro here has got a big announcement to make.'

Jethro chuckled as rushes pinged through his head. He was high, and for the first time, he sensed Lewistock was coming together, for real.

Within ten seconds, Sparky had shushed-up the entire bar. Everyone sat staring at Jethro. He began to explain. Two minutes later the pub erupted with excitement, anticipation. Questions were fired from all directions. Jethro made it clear it was open to all, to spread the word, tell everyone; the moment of their age was upon them. He was off his face and his lucent black eyes seemed to captivate the young legion of frustrated revellers, desperate for wilder times in this forgotten outpost.

Jethro's blood fizzed, pressing him to go on, to whip up a frenzy, but he only had lies left in him. 'And there's some big guest DJs confirmed.'

The kids started whooping and popping shapes with their hands as they strutted like robots around the pub.

'What DJs?' asked Ceri, an old-school junglist, a veteran of the early rave scene, who was sitting at the bar.

Everyone paused and turned back to Jethro, waiting for his response.

'Danny Slade's sorting it out, spoke to him last week, some big names from Chequers and Night Owl.' Jethro had never met Danny Slade, the pioneering DJ of the house music scene in Tenby.

The kids looked back to Ceri. He nodded approvingly. Mayhem broke out. A queue quickly gathered outside the phone box on the square, people keen to spread the news.

'We've gotta go tell Gurnard now,' insisted Sparky.

'George, can you take us to this country club please, boss?' shouted Jethro across the bar.

'Yep, I'll be there in a minute. Finish my pint.'

'Hey, you're too pissed to get behind the wheel, you fucking twat,' said Sally the barmaid, pointing sternly at George.

'The more I drinks, the better I fucking drives, Sal. You knows that,' said George. 'Come on, let's go before Glyn locks up and fucks off to bed. If we get there by half-ten, he'll be fine.'

Sally rolled her eyes. 'You be fucking careful now.'

'Steamo!' chanted George, stumbling forward out of the pub. Jethro, Biscuits, Deri and Sparky followed, amphetamines and snakebite tearing through their veins as they sucked down roll-ups to settle their energy.

George's van spluttered into action and they took off, snaking down the coast road towards the North Pembrokeshire Country Club, George fully focused, hands gripping the wheel, as the boys hollered like delirious clowns in the back.

They stumbled into the yard of the country club, drawn to the illuminated 'Restaurant' sign on the side of a plastic burger van that was parked between two cabins, billowing out the sweet smell of fried onions. Jethro struggled to focus on the words written above the ketchup stand. He squinted as he read aloud, 'This establishment has three Michelin tyres.'

'What does that mean?' asked Biscuits.

'Fuck knows,' said Sparky, assessing the van. 'It's got four fucking wheels.'

'So this is a country club, is it, George?' said Jethro.

'Aye,' said George, struggling to navigate his flame to the end of his cigarette while scuttling sideways into the darkness.

'Two fucking cabins in a farmyard with a burger van in the middle,' whispered Jethro to himself, before bursting into a fit of laughter.

'Hey, boy,' said George. 'People make a place, so don't take the fucking piss.'

'Fucking hell. I'm not, George! Seriously, this place is great.'

'Good. If you look around, you'll see all the local farmers, builders, chippies, plumbers and sparkies, all with their vans pointed in the right direction for the journey home – the Starlight Express, we calls it. It's a good job there's hedges to bounce off, cos otherwise we'd all be fucking dead by now.'

'Hiya, boys!' welcomed Gurnard, breezing down the cabin steps with a pint in each hand, his eyes wide, pupils gaping. He raised his arms carefully to give his boys Deri and Sparky a hug.

'How is it, Gurno?' sang Deri, his arm curled behind Gurnard's back.

'Fucking flying, boys. Off the head.'

Chapter 6

Mostyn had never really warmed to Boutros, but he couldn't say why. Maybe it was because he was from away. Boutros was a similar age, but they had been poles apart in their journeys through life. Mostyn was well aware of that.

Saturday night, the younger boys were out drinking around the Havens, and just Mostyn and Boutros sat at the bar of the Fat Badger while Jules popped in and out of the kitchen, flapping over the few bar meals he had to prepare. Boutros never felt the need to spark up a conversation; he would just slowly run his index finger around the rim of his pint glass and stare at the bottom shelf of spirits, conveniently in his eyeline across the bar.

'Quiet here tonight,' said Mostyn.

'Yes, it is, isn't it?' said Boutros, waking gently from his thoughts. 'It's funny, you'd expect it to be busy.'

'Everyone's down the Havens I expect. I was down in Little Haven today, stunning it was. Everyone was out drinking on the wall of the Swan and the lawn of the Castle. Lovely to see the place so alive. I expect the boys are heading to the Dru now, for sunset.'

'Of course, it will be spectacular there tonight. It makes all the difference when the sun shines down here, doesn't it? It's quite remarkable, actually. I've never seen a land that lights up so much with sunshine.'

'Aye,' said Mostyn, 'it's because it's such a bloody rare occurrence. Like an eclipse!'

They both laughed. Silence returned. Mostyn could feel Boutros's eyes flickering at him as he played with the stack of dog-eared beer mats.

'So, how's it going, Mostyn? You look troubled, old boy, if you don't mind me saying.'

Mostyn was surprised with the words as he took a long swallow from his pint glass. As he placed the glass carefully back on the bar, he took a deep breath and raised his head. 'Boutros, if the truth be told, I'm up to my nuts in troubles. Like you wouldn't believe.'

'Oh, really? Sorry to hear that, Mostyn. I can't imagine the pressures of working the land in this day and age. Shouldn't the rave next week go a long way to alleviating the problems?'

'Well, yes. Some way. But you see, I've got myself into trouble borrowing a bit of extra money.'

'Shit. You mean not from the bank?'

'Aye, from a moneylender. A local bloke. No, a local gangster, to be more precise. I actually borrowed quite a bit and it got stolen on the same day. By him, I think.'

'Bugger. Really? That's a bloody poor show.'

'Poor show. Aye, you could say that. He's paid me a visit. And yes, before you ask, these cuts and bruises are the result of that visit.'

'Dear God, Mostyn, that's awful. You can't go to the police? This shouldn't happen. It's 1994! Christ, I thought I'd left all that behind in the developing world.'

'Police? Hell no. There's no proof of anything. I'll be signing my own death warrant if I lodge a complaint at the station. That Weird Head is a bloody psychopath, and the Growler, the money man, sounds even worse.'

Boutros frowned and he slowly rolled his head, a silent prompt to tease more information from Mostyn.

'Don't ask,' said Mostyn.

'Holy shit, Mostyn,' said Frankie, pounding up to the bar. 'You look like you've just done ten rounds with Frank Bruno.' Frankie put his arm firmly around Mostyn's shoulders. 'What happened, boy?'

'It's a long story, Frankie.'

'I don't care. I'm not going anywhere and you look like death warmed up. Come on...'

Mostyn told them everything. The bank deadline, the risk of losing the farm, the moneylending, the intimidation, the suicide attempt, and about Jethro. Mostyn felt the weight slowly lift from his shoulders as he sucked the bubbly head off his third pint.

Frankie knew of Weird Head and had heard stories of the Growler, so he made no bravado promises of retaliation.

'This is serious, Mostyn,' said Frankie. 'You can't fuck about with these people.'

'I know, Frankie. I know.'

'There's been some very funny business with that Weird Head,' Frankie continued. 'You've gotta fucking watch him. His mother and father vanished a few years back, into thin air, on the same day. It was funny because they seemed quite settled here. They were treasurers of the vintage tractor club, quite pleasant, although his old man was starting to go a bit doolally. He's always claimed they went back to Cardiff to live, but it all seemed too sudden, something wasn't right. And there's talk that Weird Head's been using their credit cards at Macky's petrol station ever since they disappeared. Odd business, I tell you.'

'You saying he bumped them off?' asked Mostyn.

'I'm not saying fuck all, Mostyn. I'm just telling you what I've heard. Fuck all more. But what I am saying is that you're gonna need some ravers turning up for Lewistock next weekend to sort all this shit out, that's for sure.'

'Aye, well, that's the plan, but we've still got a long way to go,' said Mostyn, rubbing his hands. 'We need to meet with all the boys on Sunday to finalise the logistics. I have no idea what's going on, if the truth be told.'

'Excuse me, Mostyn,' said a young familiar voice from over his shoulder.

Mostyn turned around and there was Jonny, best friend of Rhys, Colwyn and Ruth's son, standing with a pool cue in his hand.

'Hiya, Jonny, how are you, boy?'

'Aye, alright thanks. Sorry to bother you, could I have a quick word, please?'

Mostyn quickly glanced at Boutros and Frankie. 'Of course, young man. Ruth and Rhys, they're alright, aren't they?'

'Aye, nothing drastic. Can we speak in private?'

'Aye, no bother. Come on, let's nip out to the beer garden then.'

Frankie and Boutros exchanged grave glances as Mostyn and Jonny meandered out through the back door of the pub.

'Jesus, Boutros. You must be wondering what you've walked into with this place, but on my life, I've never seen or heard of trouble like this in my lifetime in Little Emlyn. Poor Mostyn. He's fucked. That Weird Head has battered half the county, probably knocked off his own folks, and this Growler fella, he's a monster. He's only ever been spotted with a brown balaclava over his head in Withybush woods. He's a giant by all accounts, nearly seven foot tall. No one knows who he is, but he walks among us every day.'

'Christ,' said Boutros.

'What's up, son?' asked Mostyn.

'Sorry, but I overheard your conversation at the bar just now when I was playing pool.'

'Aye, go on.'

'Well, Rhys told me never to say anything, but I have to tell you, Mostyn.'

'It's OK, son, you can tell me anything. If it has anything to do with the safety of Colwyn's family, then please tell me. He was my best friend, Jonny, and I love his family like they're my own. Tell me, what's the matter?'

'I know those names, Weird Head and the Growler. Rhys told me about them.' Jonny paused and looked Mostyn in the eye. 'He told me they were the reason Mr Morgan killed himself.'

Mostyn stared blankly, trying to process the words. Jonny's eyes filled with water, his body was shuddering and Mostyn drew him in.

'They still visit the farm. Mrs Morgan gets threats. Rhys is terrified. He won't let me stay there anymore in case they're attacked at night. Please help, Mostyn. Please, please.'

Mostyn drew back, clasped Jonny firmly by his shoulders and stooped his head so their eyes met. 'Of course, son, of course I will. I just wish someone had told me before. I can't believe I didn't work it out myself.' Mostyn looked up at the sky and scratched his neck nervously with both hands. 'Bloody hell. Of course.'

It all made sense. Colwyn would never have taken his life just on account of his bank debt. Mostyn pictured his best friend swinging by his neck from the rafters of the shed. That gentle Adonis of a man who'd wrestled a thousand bulls, choosing to end his life as a sack of lifeless flesh and bone at the end of a rope, just to set himself free.

Mostyn had been told how Colwyn had built a meticulous staircase of straw bales that led him up to his point of self-execution, and imagined what thoughts crossed his mind as he toiled over his own suicide machine.

Colwyn was never a strong-willed or bullish man. He was quiet and dutiful, spending the little spare time he had escaping to times past, watching old movies and musicals with old-fashioned humour and happy endings. All the family knew he was a dreamer, a romantic, fuelled by nostalgia, so they allowed him his space for those few short hours every weekend without interruption or mocking.

Some days, Colwyn would skip across the yard in front of the kitchen window and attempt his Fred Astaire kicks for Ruth, even in the rain.

'You're brave, Jonny. As you heard just now in there, I'm also on the tail end of intimidation from those bastards, but I have told the boys here and we are going to sort it out together, one way or the other. No one else is going to be hurt by them. I'll go and see Ruth now and I promise you, I will let nothing bad happen to her, or Rhys. Ever. Everything is going to be fine now, Jonny, you understand?'

'Yes. Thank you, Mostyn.'

Mostyn was about to turn and leave the porch. She's probably in bed, he thought. It was getting late. He finally heard footsteps.

'Who's there?' said Ruth. 'Who's there?'

'It's Mostyn, Ruth.'

It was only after Mostyn began to stir the sugar into his tea that he broke away from the small talk.

'Ruth. I was talking to young Jonny this evening. He told me about Weird Head and the Growler.'

Ruth was still. Her face went pale.

'Ruth. Those bastards lent me money too. Then they stole it from me.'

'Oh, Mostyn, I don't know what to do. They keep ringing in the middle of the night and I keep bumping into those brutes in the shops in town. They smile at me, they even offer to help me carry my bags, but I know they're following me, they want to hurt me.'

'Now, now, Ruth, don't think like that. They are just thugs – they intimidate, that's all.' He didn't believe himself.

'You think, Mostyn? I don't know. That Weird Head came round less than two weeks after Col's funeral, offering his condolences, the bastard, and told Rhys that we still needed to pay back over sixteen thousand, otherwise he would start repossessing our property. He said he'd give us a month to start repayments, but we've got nothing. Poor Rhys is out there day and night now, just like his father was, just trying to make ends meet for us. The boy is terrified. He still needs his father. I don't know what to do.'

Mostyn pulled his chair close to Ruth and put his arm around her and held her as she wept.

'We could sell everything, but then what? Rhys was born to farm. He's been out there every day since he was five years old helping his dad.'

'I know, Ruth. It shouldn't have to come to that. Have you spoken to Mr Price lately? Maybe the bank can give you a bit of leeway until Rhys finds his feet.'

'Yes, I met with him last week. He's such an odd little man. So fidgety. He can't make eye contact at all. I can't stand that. And those high heels he wears to make himself look taller. Bloody ridiculous. He said our credit line has run out. Apparently "Head Office" has tightened up financing for small farms that are struggling. We've borrowed as much as we can.'

'Aye, he told me the same. I've got a big deadline to meet at the end of the month. If I don't make that, I'll have to sell up.'

They were both quiet for a moment. The grating metallic tick of the grandfather clock filled the silent room.

'Sometimes I think dying would be a relief.'

'Stop that now, Ruth, please. You've got a young man out there who needs his mother, who's got his whole life ahead of him. He's going to struggle as it is, so please don't talk like that.'

'I know, I'm sorry. Talking bloody stupid, I am.'

'I understand, girl. It's crossed my mind too.'

'It's the loneliness. That's what makes it so unbearable. I've never felt this alone in my life, Mostyn. After all these years.'

'Aye. I suppose I've been used to it for so long now. But please know I'm here for you and Rhys whenever you need me, Ruth.'

They held each other's gaze without discomfort.

Mostyn and Ruth had courted long before she and Colwyn had met. They were just youngsters, around six years old, when they were put next to each other in Sunday school in Little Emlyn chapel. Ruth's family farm, Bramble Rock, was three miles outside the parish, near Roch. The friendship blossomed in their late teens, fuelled by their mutual love of horse riding.

In the hot summer of 1948, they would meet each month during full moon for a night gallop out to the coast. Mostyn would tell his parents he was going to visit his Aunty Peggy, who was in on the bluff. He would disappear into the dusk, charging through the bursting hedgerows down to Bramble Rock. Ruth would wait at the bottom of the lane having sold a similar tale, and they would gallop over the long brow of the ancient coastline that finally descended onto the golden sands of Newgale and to the Atlantic Ocean, where it seemed to them as if they had reached the end of the world.

'Remember those nights we galloped to Newgale, Most?'

'Huh! Aye, how could I forget!'

'Do you know what I remember the most?' asked Ruth.

'The moonlight on the sea as the swell lines rolled in? That's what I remember,' said Mostyn softly, but what he saw in his memory was the moonlight in Ruth's blue eyes, how the salty breeze had drawn out the soft red glow from her weathered cheeks, and the lips he'd yearned to kiss.

'The smells, the honeysuckle, the freshly cut silage, the hay dust. Then the warm breeze of the sea as we dropped down the hill. We were so alive!' Ruth smiled, still deep in their history.

Mostyn studied her face and remembered the day he was told to never come over to Bramble Rock again. It was the day of Gareth's funeral. The young boy, his little brother, five years old, had wandered off while the family were bringing cows home from the field for sorting. For two desperate days the family and villagers searched the fields, woods and rivers day and night for the boy. He was found at nightfall, by his father, at the bottom of the slurry pit, having slipped through a broken fence on the bank above it that was long due to be fixed.

Gilbert, Mostyn's father, waded in to retrieve the corpse of his youngest son. The previous week, Gilbert had caught him playing around the broken fence and yelled at him to keep away. But he could see this warning only served to fuel the boy's intrigue. His regret for not mending that fence, a one-hour job, was immeasurable.

Gilbert had clung to the hope that Gareth had wandered off and was seeking refuge in one of the many deep woods that surrounded Lewis Mill. But after two days, Gilbert turned away from the search party in the west wood at dusk, strode back through the farmyard and waded into the stinking slurry pit. He knew the place where his son would be lying, directly below the broken fence on the high bank above.

The silhouette of his father, mummified in muck, wading out of the pit at sundown with the lifeless toddler in his arms, his brother, his only sibling, travelled with Mostyn and appeared whenever there was darkness. Every night, every time he closed his eyes, it returned.

Gilbert, Mary and Mostyn were ostracised from much of the farming community of Little Emlyn and beyond after Gareth's death. It was an unwritten rule that every farmer had a duty to protect his children from the potential perils of the working farm, and Gilbert had failed. As Mostyn left the church after the burial, he felt a firm hand grip his right shoulder. It was Mr Griffiths, Ruth's father. He'd pulled Mostyn close. 'I'm very sorry for your loss, Mostyn, but I think it's time you stopped visiting Ruth and spent more time at home. Your parents will need you now, no doubt.' There was no compassion. It was the final blow.

'Are you alright, Most?' asked Ruth.

'Aye. Aye. Sorry, I was just thinking about Gareth.'

Their weathered eyes met again.

'My father was a good man deep down, Most. He really was.'

'I don't doubt that, Ruth. Not at all. It's just funny how things turn out and how paths go here and there.'

Ruth lifted her arm and gently rested her hand on Mostyn's cheek.

His chair squeaked as it slid back quickly on the slate. He stood up. 'Right, I gotta go. I've got a busy weekend ahead. I'd best be off, Ruth.'

Ruth stood up and stepped silently into Mostyn. She held his face with both hands and kissed him softly on the lips for the first time in her life. There were tears on her face. 'I'm sorry, Mostyn.'

'Don't be silly, girl. We've had a great life really, up until recently. There's no need for apologies. It's just the way things were. We'll be alright, Ruth. Just don't forget I'm here for you.'

'Thank you, my love.'

'No, thank you, Ruth. This is the nicest *cwtch* I've had for a long time.' Mostyn held Ruth close again and smiled, rubbing his hands reassuringly up and down her back. 'I'll go and see that Weird Head tomorrow and tell him to back off until after the, er...'

'After the what, Most? The rave?'

Mostyn pulled back and frowned at Ruth. 'What you on about?'

'Don't you bloody try and fool me, boy. How long have you lived in Little Emlyn?'

'Shit.'

'Don't worry, only a few people know, but word is getting around. What the hell are you doing, Mostyn?'

'Christ knows. But it's the only hope I've got, girl.'

After the service, the congregation shuffled into the vestry and the gossip began. It always started with Joyce, the eyes and ears of Little Emlyn. But, unusually, she scurried around, hushing people to wait until Minister Brown had left for his next service to begin their weekly chatter of village rumour and speculation.

Mr Brown breezed in for his customary black tea and two custard creams and cracked his old biscuit joke about rich teas being the best Baptists (something to do with dunking) to the two unsuspecting hikers who seemed to have lost their way on the Trust path, drifted in through the doors and across the pew that ended with smelly old Mowbray Codd. They drank their tea quickly and left. Mr Brown followed them out of the back door soon after, as flustered as ever.

Jim Bevan rolled his eyes. 'One bloody day a week he works, and look at him flappin'. And he gets his Sunday dinner cooked for him as well.'

'Aye. The man's a bloody genius,' said Joyce. 'Only fools and horses work, boy. Look at you. Back's as bent as a butcher's hook, and what bloody for?'

Jim frowned and looked out onto the road as Mr Brown grinned and waved, then sped off up the road in his shiny new red Rover 216s, paid for by the chapel.

'Bastard,' he whispered.

'So what's this all about Mostyn having a rave up at Lewis Mill then?' said Joyce. 'Jim, you must know what's going on. You see him nearly every day.'

'I do, but it's funny these days. Since Col left us, poor old Mostyn just hasn't been himself. He doesn't come to the mart anymore and you know we haven't seen him in here since the funeral. He seems to spend more time down the pub than anywhere. I've seen him with this young boy in his Land Rover a few times, can't be more than eighteen, nineteen I should think. Towny type, not a farm boy, that's for sure. It's all a bit strange.'

'Poor Mostyn,' said Mary the organist. 'Him and Col were close. It can't be easy. And with all the problems and changes nowadays, it must be tough for the poor old boy.'

'Aye, you're right there, Mary,' said Jim. 'Things are changing, quickly. Everything's getting bigger and faster. Just take the harvest these past weeks. Those bloody subcontractors are moving in with their monster tractors and blitzing the fields overnight. They drive like bloody maniacs. All you see at night now are light beams in the fields, combining and baling in the dark. It's bloody wrong. It's killing farming. The harvest should be a time to bring everyone together, throw a few bales, drink some cider, the kids riding on the top of the stacks down the lanes. It's all bloody disappearing.'

'Yes,' said Mary, 'couldn't agree more. I'm not being funny, but it's all going to hell. Serious. Look at the kids, they don't play out anymore, always on those bloody computer games. None of them want to build a den in the hay or go to Sunday school, and the trouble is, none of us are forcing them to. My boys tell me to piss off if I tell them to do anything, and if I get my wooden spoon out, they're on the phone to Esther bloody Rantzen.'

The gathering all nodded woefully.

'This rave is going ahead, two weeks yesterday,' chipped in Boutros. He could see the conversation needed a boost.

The talking stopped and all eyes turned to him.

'How do you know that, Nigel?' asked Joyce, clearly put out.

'Well, I'm helping Mostyn, along with a few other boys from the pub.'

'Like who?' asked Jim.

'John the Ghost, Chicken George and Frankie, mostly, and Jules and myself are helping where we can.'

'Well, hell, there's a bloody set!' said Joyce between laughs.

'Does Mostyn know what he's letting himself in for?' asked Jim. 'Those ravers are like zombies. I saw a documentary about it last week. The drugs they take. It's all hell let loose. Why on Earth is he doing it?'

'To raise some money to clear some debts,' said Boutros. 'Simple as that. He's got it bloody tough at the moment. A few things hang in the balance. If he can generate a few thousand quid with that rave, it will help a lot. If it fails, then, well...' Boutros pulled back.

'It's all very well trying to make some money, there's nothing wrong with that, but those ravers will terrorise us all,' said Mary. 'They'll be breaking into our houses and stealing everything to pay for all that ecstasy. I've been reading about it for years now. They're all possessed.'

'Now that's probably not true, Mary,' Boutros responded. 'The boy organising it is Jethro Jones. He's from Neyland. His father was that man who fell off the bridge and sadly passed away.'

'Oh, terribly sad story that. Poor old Trev the Brush,' said Joyce.

'Aye,' muttered the others.

'You all probably shouldn't believe everything you read in the papers,' continued Boutros. 'I'm not saying these ravers aren't to be ignored, but from what I understand, most of them around here are just the normal kids in the sixth form, or from Pembrokeshire College. Students, most of them.'

'Yes, but it's the drugs, Nigel. They change people,' said Mary.

'Mary, they're not all on drugs. It's just the few who tarnish things for the majority. It's always like that.'

Everyone raised their eyebrows and looked around at one another, unconvinced.

'OK, look. At the end of the day, it's Mostyn's business, not ours. It's on his land, a long way from the village, so I don't think any of you have anything to worry about. And I know some of you,' he said, nodding towards Joyce, 'would even like to help. But the biggest contribution you could all make, to be brutally honest, is just to keep it secret from the wider community, and of course from anyone related to the police.'

The chirping began again, bouncing around the musty walls of the vestry. Boutros sensed a nervous energy fill the room. He knew the rave was the most exciting event ever to be held in Little Emlyn. And the fact it was illegal only fuelled the intrigue of the parishioners, many of whom had drifted through the past decades with blinkers on.

Boutros could see Joyce was so wound up that, if allowed, she would likely spin out of the vestry door and pirouette through the graveyard screaming 'RAAAAAVE!' at the top of her voice. He caught her attention and put his finger to his lips, raised his eyebrows and winked. She shot back a scout's honour salute and darted out through the back door.

Mowbray Codd had been sitting at the back of the vestry taking it all in, without a hint of participation. Boutros had clocked that. His diplomatic instinct sensed a snitch. He nodded his way, and Mowbray nodded back soberly.

Chapter 7

The old car started, as usual, with the first turn of the key. It was Boutros's pride and joy. Whenever he returned from a mission, the first thing he and Dolly would do would be to go for a spin from their home in Old Amersham out into the Chilterns. The roar of that vintage Mercedes engine down the lanes to Little Missenden signalled to Boutros that he was home, where he belonged, in his England.

He pulled into the yard. Jethro and Biscuits sat up, startled, and stared.

'Wow, nice wheels,' said Biscuits, dreamily.

'That is beautiful,' said Jethro, equally entranced.

Boutros parked up and stepped out of the car, smooth as cream in a white linen suit, matching Panama hat, and multicoloured stripes running vertically through his shirt, making him look even taller and more genteel.

'Morning, chaps. Nigel Green, chauffeur extraordinaire, reporting for duty.' He tipped his hat and flashed a wry smirk.

'Alright,' said Jethro. 'Nice car. Really nice car. What is it?'

'It's a 280 SEL to be precise, young man. 1970. The actual car used at the Geneva Motor Show. We bought it the year we married. Smashing car, lots of memories.'

Biscuits could sense them hurtling through Boutros's mind in the short moment he smiled back at the car. He was intrigued by the old man, and impressed with his look. Biscuits liked a bit of class. He loved The Jam, the tailored suits, but would never attempt to dress in such a way in Neyland. He'd be slaughtered, he was sure.

To Biscuits, Boutros was just the posh bloke, the old ornament that sat at the bar of the Fat Badger, and he was concerned about riding in his car for the next hour. He hated awkward moments with strangers. His dad used to leave him in pubs as a child, and often on away matches. Forgotten most of the time, but always cared for by kind folk. The humiliation of being pitied by strangers never left him.

What is he doing with us? Biscuits asked himself, as this elegant old Englishman opened the back door of his beautiful car for him to step into. Is he taking the piss? But the smell of vintage class soon enveloped him as he sank into the back seat and discreetly bobbed on its springs. Red leather, cream stitching. He imagined himself into the frames of an old movie.

Jethro sat in the front. He knew it would be a difficult journey. Biscuits and Boutros, chalk and cheese.

They pulled out of the yard and hit early morning traffic within five hundred yards. John Hughes, waddling up Lewisdale Hill, following his herd of ten or twelve cows with their freshly emptied udders and joyfully slapping each side of their underbellies as they lumbered and lurched their way up the hill and back into the field.

'You sure you don't mind taking us around Tenby this week, Boutros?' said Jethro.

'Not at all.'

'Honestly, we can get the bus from town. It's no trouble. We don't want to put you out. Surely you must have better things to do?'

'Er, no. I don't, as a matter of fact.'

'So how did you end up down here then?' asked Biscuits.

'Well, my wife and I, we decided to retire here. I've been coming to Pembrokeshire since I was a child. My parents loved it here and made some friends in the Havens around the time of the war.'

'So where are you from exactly?' asked Jethro.

'Amersham, Buckinghamshire. About an hour and a half north-west of London.'

The boys made an 'Ahh' sound and lifted their heads and eyebrows in unison. Boutros smiled.

'Doesn't your wife mind you spending the week with two nineteen-year-old ravers?' quizzed Biscuits.

Jethro dropped his eyelids.

'No, young man, she doesn't. She's dead.'

'Oh, shit, I'm sorry. I didn't know. I'm really sorry.'

'That's OK. You weren't to know. That's life, squire.' Boutros raised his head to look directly into his rear-view mirror and studied the boy on his back seat. Looks a bit shrivelled, thought Boutros, like an unwatered flower just after its bloom. 'So what do you do, Biscuits, is it?'

'Er, not a lot. Bits and bobs, odds and sods. I'm probably gonna try and get on to a GNVQ course next year.'

'What's that?'

'Er, I'm not too sure exactly what it means. It's like A levels, but you can focus on a subject or a job you like or might want to do.'

'More vocational, like an apprenticeship?'

'Aye. That's the one.'

'So, what do you want to be when you grow up, young man?' thundered Boutros.

'I dunno.'

'Really? You have no idea?'

'Nope.'

'What do you like?'

'Dunno. I read a bit, but I suppose music is my thing.'

'Well, that's a start. There are lots of opportunities in the music industry, particularly in London. Working in music studios, West End productions, the film industry. In fact, my old neighbour in Amersham used to arrange some of the musical sequences on *The Wombles*.'

Biscuits laughed. He felt enlightened and positive as the car tanked past Haverfordwest Golf Club. He observed the men on the fairways, having never considered them in his life before. They looked relaxed and happy. I'd like to do that one day, he thought, as they disappeared out of sight.

Boutros accelerated up Arnolds Hill, overtaking four sets of cars and caravans that had crawled to a near standstill near the top.

'So what was your job?' asked Biscuits.

'Oh, I just used to work for the United Nations.'

'Just!' exclaimed Jethro. 'That must have been amazing.'

'Well, it depends which way you look at it, I suppose,' said Boutros thoughtfully.

'Didn't you live all over the world?' asked Jethro.

'Yes, I spent most of my working life on mission. Although I had an office in Geneva, most of my time was spent in the field.'

'So where have you lived?' asked Biscuits.

'Ooof, blimey. South and South-East Asia mostly, I suppose.'

'What countries is that?'

'India. I spent a lot of time in India. Burma, Cambodia, Laos, Vietnam, then back to the Arabian Peninsula for a few years. I'm bloody old. I've spent a long time all over the place.'

'What was your job?' Biscuits' imagination was unleashed.

'Well, I started when I was in my early twenties, straight from university. Somehow I landed a job in Geneva, at the World Health Organization, just as a junior officer. Then I worked my way up to managing projects, helping communities with health problems. Not nice stuff really. The last few years I was mostly working with people affected by AIDS. But it's all too grim and boring for you two to listen to.'

'No, keep going, I want to hear about it,' said Biscuits. 'I've only been to England twice. Tell us some stories about the places you've lived?'

'Like what?'

'I dunno.' Biscuits paused, racking his brain for a line of enquiry. 'What's the worst thing you ever experienced?'

Boutros bobbed his head around for a moment and twitched his nose from side to side, then fell silent. Jethro slowly turned his head towards Biscuits. They both felt the tension begin to cut into them.

Boutros raised his eyes and considered Biscuits again. He looked so naive and ignorant, yet he found his stream of questions and the way he delivered them charming and interesting.

'One of the worst things that stands out in my mind was seeing this young girl, no more than six years old, about the same age as my daughter, Maggie, at that time, come running up to me on the platform in Calcutta train station. This is back in, let me see, 1978, I think. As she approached me, I could see something truly disturbing in her eyes. I could see she had leprosy. Both her eyelids had been eaten away, as had part of her lips. She couldn't blink and these big bulging eyeballs just glared at me like I was face to face with the living dead. A child. She was utterly distraught, pulling at my shirt, pointing up the platform. I'd worked at several leper centres, but I hadn't expected to see this little girl at this moment. I'd seen death and despair in the most horrific conditions, for decades. But it was all on my daily planning, my work, my job, so I could prepare myself. Disengage.

'I'd just woken up from a very long ride, all the way from Madras in the south. It was supposed to be an express train, but it turned out to be a mail train, and stopped at every bloody village on the way. Was supposed to take thirty-six hours, but it took fifty-four. Three bloody days! Imagine. And the toilets. Goodness gracious me, they were something else. The last day I just had to stick my behind in from the corridor to do my business. It was overflowing. A mound of poop. The smell. It's never left me.'

The boys cringed.

'Anyway, I get off the train, dazed, confused, tired, like you can't imagine. It's around 5am. And there to meet me is this little girl, with no eyelids. Her gums half visible. Her head like a warm skull patched up with flesh.' Boutros wriggled up in his seat and the boys leaned secretly towards him. 'I go with her, up the platform, snaking against the flow of people, a sea of humanity right there, even before the sun had risen. We stop at a bench. She looks at me and then she looks down. There's a mess of blankets. She pulls them back and there's her mother. Dead. Rotten with the same disease, only much worse, if you can imagine that. Her face like a bloodied intestine. Like roadkill. Her eyes were frozen open with an expression of pain that she surely carried into eternity.

'Oh, pull over, you bloody bastard!' Boutros cursed at the tractor and trailer bumbling slowly in front of him. The boys bolted upright, their minds suspended in Calcutta.

As they accelerated off Kilgetty roundabout a few minutes later, Boutros overtook, then slowed with the clear road to Tenby ahead of them.

'So, what happened to the girl?' asked Biscuits.

'Well, it's not a happy ending, let's put it that way. Like most lives in the developing world, things start off all bells and whistles, growing up on a tropical beach, a pristine jungle. Chasing chickens at sunrise, playing cricket at sunset. But the looming world of work, effort, physical suffering and illness is only a few short years down the track. By eight, nine, ten years old, most kids are workhorses, shoved into the corners of sweathouses and factories. This is their life, every day, for decades. Exposed to pollution, poisons, disease, unsafe conditions.'

'Yeah, but what happened to the girl?' insisted Jethro.

'I put the covers back over her mother's face and held her hand. We walked down to a small food stall at the back of one of the platforms and I ordered her a freshly pressed orange juice and an omelette. We sat together for about thirty minutes and I genuinely felt my heart aching. The only time in my life, except for when Dolly left me. I imagined my little Maggie with leprosy, alone in the world in this unforgiving place. The little girl was already dead. She knew it. At six bloody years old.' He paused. 'Where are we going to park?'

'There's loads of parking in Tenby, Boutros,' said Jethro. 'Just follow the signs to the town centre, still a few miles to go. The girl! What happened to her?'

'I left her.'

'What? Just there, with her omelette?' asked Biscuits.

'Yes. Just there, with her omelette. I gave her fifty rupees. She didn't even say thank you. She just said, "More! More!" I gave her another fifty. She said, "More! More!"'

They sat in silence.

'But I'm quite sure she did it on purpose,' Boutros continued softly.

'What?' quizzed Biscuits.

'The "More! More!" I believe to this day that she could see the helplessness in me. And she knew she was dying. I think her compassion for me was even greater than mine for her. I couldn't save her. She could see I was desperate to help, but she knew deep down it was all in vain. She knew my heart was needlessly breaking for her so she put an end to it by pushing me away. She set me free in the end.'

Boutros swung his head sideways and offered a melancholy smile to Jethro, but he didn't respond; he looked ahead.

'The selfless dignity of that young human soul shone through in that pit of Calcutta on that morning and touched me like nothing did before or has ever since. She will be with me when I draw my last breath.'

'What was her name?' asked Jethro.

'Anjali. Which means "gift" in Hindi.'

Silence filled the car again. Biscuits frowned and massaged his left earlobe for a long moment as he stared out at the building traffic as they approached the outskirts of Tenby. 'So surely meeting Anjali was the best thing you ever experienced?'

Boutros huffed through his nose approvingly. 'Yes, I suppose you're right, Biscuits.'

Their eyes met in the mirror and Boutros winked warmly at him.

'So what's the worst thing you ever experienced then?'

'Jesus, Biscuits. Give us all a break, will you? For fuck's sake,' said Jethro.

Boutros chuckled. He loved the energy and naivety of the two boys, how their characters sparked off one another. He wanted to continue.

'The worst, worst thing? That's easy,' said Boutros.

'Go on,' said Jethro.

'Myself.'

'What do you mean?'

'The worst thing I've ever seen is myself,' said Boutros, matter-of-factly.

'Sorry. I'm lost,' said Biscuits, shuffling upright in his seat again, intrigued.

'The worst thing I have ever seen in all my days is myself, the day of my retirement. They threw a big party for me in the delegate's restaurant in the Palais des Nations.'

'Sounds posh.'

'Oh, it is. But so clogged with stuffiness and dead wood you can hardly breathe. Anyway, my boss was giving a nice speech about my service and achievements and all I could think was, "What a load of bollocks." It was all puffed-up stretched truths. Smoke and mirrors. Turd polishing. I caught a glimpse of myself in a mirror and I just stared. "Who are you?" I thought. I looked around at all the strange people there, many of them I'd known for years, and wondered, "Who the hell are all you lot?" At that moment, it dawned on me that through all of my professional life, I'd pretty much been a phoney. Drifting around the world, not keeping any real cohesive friendships, and not really achieving anything myself. Filling in forms, mostly. Ticking boxes. Telling people where to stand. I was just part of that big back-slapping UN machine that takes credit for all the good being done in the world, bragging about it at dinner parties, when the reality was and still is much different.'

'What do you mean?' asked Biscuits.

'Well, it's the bloody locals who do all the real work, like anywhere. Nurses, doctors, the volunteers. And the money wasting, the time wasting. Dear God, it still makes me want to vomit.'

Biscuits' head was pushed back on the rear seat as he listened. 'So the UN is a load of shit then, is it?'

'Well, no, not complete and utter shit. It's good it's there, don't get me wrong, but it could just be so much better if everyone tried harder. And in the end, I literally felt embarrassed in my skin turning up to countries like Vietnam and Laos, who'd not long had the living shit bombed out of them by white men for years. Then there's me telling them how they should rebuild their communities in my pressed chinos, baby-blue shirt and with my clipboard. Jesus.' Boutros tutted and shook his head.

'Sounds like you're being a bit harsh on yourself, Boutros,' said Jethro.

'No, not really. Not at all, in fact. I'm too old and weathered to be anything but honest, Jethro. And another thing you young men should know that is very important: I've come to realise since moving down here that I was bereft of community all my life until I landed in Pembrokeshire and the Fat Badger.'

'What does that mean?' asked Biscuits.

'I was missing community. In fact, I never had it. In my sixty-eight years on this planet, the only time I felt a sense of belonging, like I was part of and cared for like a community member, was when I met Frankie and the boys in the pub and the kind folks in the chapel after I lost my wife.'

'Really?' Jethro sounded amazed.

'Yep. All my life I've travelled, visited communities all over the world, observing as an outsider. At the time I considered many of those communities to be backwards, even weird, but it turns out I was the bloody weirdo. A travelling, rootless white man drifting in and out of cultures that I had no common ground, connection or affinity with.'

'That was just part of your job though, wasn't it?' said Jethro.

'Yes, it was, but I see now that I wasted decades of my life. Always away from my family. Missing out on my kids' upbringing, sports days, cricket matches on summer afternoons, picking them up when they fell. All that cliché nonsense, which actually turns out to be true. I only bloody realised it recently, when it was too late. So don't make the same mistakes as I did, chaps.'

'Well, I can't wait to get the fuck out of here,' said Jethro.

'Me too,' said Biscuits.

'Really? Why is that?' asked Boutros.

By the time the car had parked up, less than an hour after three near-strangers had jumped in, three friends stepped out, a unit, ready to implement the groundwork for the biggest rave Pembrokeshire had ever seen.

The fourth week of August was the climax of the summer season. Droves of locals and tourists would descend on this quintessential Welsh seaside town with its panoramic white sand beaches and antiquated cobbled streets. Peak season never failed to rattle the senses as Tenby swelled. Voracious seagulls, screaming children, the whirl of fruit machines, the soundtrack to the motion of seething streets and cluttered beaches.

But between the cracks of this kiss-me-quick town, a movement was simmering. Movers and shakers. Old dogs. The usual suspects. Bedrooms transformed into training camps for warm-up sets and after-parties. A guerrilla army stocked with amplifiers, tinsel and an artillery of vinyl that was traded more briskly on the back streets than buckets and spades on North Beach. The scene was all-consuming and contagious, hypnotising its flock with ecstasy and progressive beats that seeped into the veins and throbbed in the chests of the converted. It grew through the clubs, Chequers and the Night Owl, cosmic wonderlands through the dilated eyes of the young uninhibited sexual souls that just wanted to dance, to hug, to fuck. The scene was new. Not a mean feat. And it never would be again, and this was sensed.

By mid-afternoon, the flyers had all been distributed. Jethro was relieved – the reaction was positive. There was only one problem. Jethro knew beforehand that two nineteen-year-olds and a colonial dinosaur were not the hippest rave salesmen for this hip town, so he ensured the bait was the flyer itself, which read:

Whirl-Y-Tribe Promotions presents: Lewistock, Field of Dreams, DJs Jon of the Pleased Wimmin and Danny Slade, This Saturday Night/Sunday. Meeting point Canaston Bowl, 1.30am, Sunday 28th August.

Jethro had made Whirl-Y-Tribe up, putting together the Whirl-Y-Gig, a psychedelic club he pined to go to in London, and the Spiral Tribe, a free party sound system that was causing mayhem with illegal raves all over England.

News of Lewistock reached Tenby House around the same time Jethro, Biscuits and Boutros arrived for a pint. Whispers and glances. A small gathering of young clubbers, smartly dressed, congregated at the bar as the news spread. The odd set of Boutros, clad like the Man from Del Monte, flanked by two scraggly teen ravers intrigued the gathering.

A boy walked over. 'Alright.'

'Alright,' said Jethro.

'Is it you organising this rave on Saturday?'

'Yep.'

'Really?'

'Yep. We're part of a collective, Whirl-Y-Tribe. We go around doing raves.'

'Never heard of them.'

'Really? We operate up north mostly, Fishguard, St David's way. Quieter up there.' Jethro surprised himself as he winked confidently at the boy. 'This is the first time we've tried to pull a crowd from Tenby.'

'So where is it exactly?'

'Little Emlyn.'

'Ha! Really? That little shitkicker village with the rubbish football team?'

'Yep, that's the one.'

'How did you get Jon Pleased confirmed for that? Or is that just bullshit?'

'Er, course not.' Jethro began to stumble.

Boutros was ready and stepped in. 'Hello, young man, my name is Nigel. I'm one of the founders of Whirl-Y-Tribe.'

They shook hands.

'We started in Goa in the seventies, in fact. We then went to Vietnam, to Nha Trang after the war and now we've all returned to the UK. Huge problems with HIV now in those places. Free love can have a high price. We lost too many. So we're back in Blighty.'

The boy nodded, eyes wide.

'We're expecting a few thousand at Lewistock next weekend. It will be the biggest underground rave Pembrokeshire has ever seen.' Boutros paused, adjusted his hat and continued with a whisper, 'So get the word around to all the girls and boys, there's a good chap, but keep it on the down-low. Interpol have had us on their radar for over fifteen years. You know what I'm saying?' Boutros put his arm around the boy and smiled graciously.

'Wow. Of course,' said the boy, scanning the pub for secret agents. 'Fucking check that out, boys,' said Buzzy.

Dean and Tommo stopped shovelling the chips and beans into their drunken, droopy mouths, raised their heads and looked out across the road. The dim light of the street lamps over Neyland high street made everything glow a warm sepia. The vinegar steam wafting up from Dean's polystyrene tray made him flinch as he and Tommo gazed at the vintage Mercedes Benz as if it were a mirage.

'That's a fucking beauty,' said Dean.

'Fuck aye,' said Tommo.

'Check out the old cunt behind the wheel,' said Buzzy.

'Great day, boys,' said Jethro.

'Was indeed,' said Boutros.

'More of the same tomorrow, then?' said Biscuits.

'Aye, but we'll focus on South Beach and Saundersfoot,' said Jethro.

'Sweet,' said Biscuits. He stepped out of the car and exchanged farewells.

'Dean, that's fucking Biscuits getting out there,' said Tommo.

'Can't be,' said Dean.

'It fucking is,' exclaimed Buzzy.

'What the fuck is that little shitbag doing in a car with that old queer?' said Tommo excitedly. 'He must be his fag. Ha! Jesus, Dean. That's your fuckin' boy.'

Dean blinked quickly, trying to focus his sloshing eyes. He saw his son, but Biscuits didn't see him across the street. Buzzy and Tommo went on, but Dean didn't hear the words. He watched his son, his long curly hair bobbing around, his hooded top decked with flowers. Fucking flowers. Baggy trousers, like a fucking faggot. Bouncing up the street. An embarrassment. A fucking embarrassment.

'Look at the way he's mincing up the street, Dean,' said Tommo. 'He must have an arse like a Japanese fuckin' flag.'

Buzzy dropped half of his chips as he buckled with laughter.

'Fuck off, Tommo, or I'll fucking do you,' said Dean. He set off after his son.

Biscuits reached up to hang his coat on the hook and the front door swung open. Dean strode in, clenched his right hand around the neck of Biscuits' top and twisted it tight to his throat.

'What? What?' said Biscuits, his eyes blazing as his father drove him against the side of the staircase. 'What have I fucking done, Dad?' he yelled.

Dean stared into him. Biscuits could find no connection. He began to whimper.

'You little fucking faggot,' whispered Dean through the grit of his teeth. 'What the fuck do you look like? How dare you walk around here dressed like that after all the fucking money I've spent on you. You trying to embarrass me, boy? Eh? And who was that old fucking faggot in that poncy car? Eh? Who? Who?'

'He's just an old English bloke, drinks in the pub in Little Emlyn. Helping us, he is. Just helping Jethro to organise this rave next weekend.'

'Rave? Fucking rave?' His voice grew louder. 'I didn't raise you to be one of those dancing fucking faggots on ecstasy.'

'I, I—'

'You trying to make me a fucking laughing stock in front of my friends, boy?' Dean twisted the fabric tighter. Biscuits began to choke.

Biscuits shoved his father and Dean fell backwards, pulling Biscuits down onto the floor with him. Dean snarled and threw his head at his son's face. Biscuits' nose cracked. Dean pulled him up and dragged him through to the kitchen, his hands around his son's neck. Blood splattered onto the walls and carpet as Biscuits tried to free himself.

Dean slammed the hallway door shut.

'Shut up, you little faggot. Stop fucking screaming.' He slapped Biscuits around the face, two, three times. 'Fucking shut up.' He grabbed him by the throat. 'Stop!'

A switch went off in Biscuits' head. His screaming stopped. Biscuits glanced down. His father's ashtray lay on the draining board next to him. His hand smashed down on it like a robotic claw and without a break in movement he drove it into the side of his father's head.

The dull crack reverberated around the room. Dean's hand released Biscuits' throat and he dropped onto the cold lino floor. He made no noise as blood seeped from the deep gash into his dirty blond hair, flowing thinly behind his ears and down the front of his face. Biscuits dropped the ashtray and loomed over his father's body for a long minute, glaring down as he hyperventilated, his bloodied nose dripping onto his father's back.

He looked up and walked calmly across the room, opened a cupboard door, reached in and took out a packet of bourbon creams, then went to the cutlery draw just below for a small peeling knife. He whipped the knife through the top of the packet and the top biscuit flipped back, hanging by a delicate hinge in its plastic hammock. He went down onto his knees, put the biscuit into his mouth and began to crunch down on it. He ran his fingers over his father's head, felt the break in his skull.

Biscuits stood up, reached for a tea towel and scrunched it over his nose to stop the bleeding, then walked back into the hallway and calmly dialled 999.

Chapter 8

It was the quietest lunchtime in the Fat Badger for weeks. A Monday, and, rarely for a summer's day, only locals blessed the bar. Jules on the taps, John the Ghost and Chicken George, and Joyce sat in between them. A storm was approaching to wash out the day.

'Dew, dew, it's emptying out there, boys,' said George, as they all allowed the beers to percolate into their brains as the rain swept in from the sea.

Joyce didn't get out much. She had to care for her elderly mother who lived with her, it was just the two of them, but now and again her sister, Hilary, came down from Anglesey to stay to give Joyce a break for a day or two. Joyce would be in the pub by noon to indulge in Jules's gammon, egg, pineapple and chips, washed down with copious amounts of her poison – Babycham Velvet, a pokey cocktail of sparkly Babycham and Guinness.

'What you doing there, boy?' asked Joyce, frowning at George. He was concentrating so hard his nose almost touched the piece of paper he was sketching on.

'Creating the future of urinals, Joyce,' he said, deadly serious.

'What you on about?'

'I've invented this thing, the Pissball Wizard, but I've still not quite perfected it.'

'You're wasting your time,' said John the Ghost. 'It's a shit idea.'

'Steady on there now, John,' said Joyce, 'give the boy a chance.' She turned back to George. 'What is it then, Georgie?'

'Just a kind of game for blokes to play when they're having a piss. Bit like a pinball machine.' George slid his design across the bar for everyone to see and spent five minutes, animated like a Blue Peter presenter, explaining the mechanics of the urinal mat with its piss-powered hollow steel ball that required blasting up through pinball machine-like plastic flaps, a simple sort of maze, into a hole at the top. George's only problem, he explained, was getting the ball to roll back and pop up into its starting position for the next urinating client.

'I likes that!' exclaimed Joyce. 'Hells bells, you're some fucking boy, George. It's genius. Can you design one for fannies?'

Jules spat out his wine and soda and John nearly fell off his stool. George reined in his laughter and continued, pushing the Pissball Wizard's many benefits – more piss in the pan, less on the floor. Marketing opportunities for advertisers who could put their ads on the game mat, brainwashing the half-cut punters with their products as they spent between forty and seventy seconds – George had done his research – staring down into the pan as they relieved themselves. He could even offer companies the chance to design their own Pissball Wizard game to suit their brand. Maybe it would prove so popular that blokes would drink more, just to go back and have another crack at conquering the Wizard.

The opportunities were endless.

'I've just gotta get that fucking ball to pop back up,' said George, shaking his head, deep in contemplation.

'Just put a box of latex gloves above the urinals, George. Then the punters can put it back themselves. Easy,' said John the Ghost, smirking.

George sat up. 'Why are you always pissing on my fires, you whinging hippy?'

'You know why. And I'd rather be a whinging hippy than a village fucking idiot. You don't help yourself with these pathetic ideas, Georgie.'

'You just fucking wait,' said George, wagging his drunken finger right in front of Joyce's nose at John the Ghost. 'Once I've nailed the design, which won't be long now, I can get them made in China for less than twenty-five pence each, and sell them for three or four quid a piece, easy. Do you know how many urinals there are just in all the pubs in the UK? Not to mention all the museums, train stations and hospitals.'

'No. How many?'

'I don't know the exact number, you twat, but there's thousands of them.'

'Who do you know in China?'

'I've got contacts.'

'Yeah, you've got the phone number of the Dragon and Pearl in town. Maybe they can deliver a truckload of Pissball Wizards with your pineapple fried rice next Sunday night.'

'For fuck's sake, will you both just shut the fuck up?' squeaked Jules. 'You're doing my bloody head in. At each other like a couple of bitches every day. And poor Joyce here doesn't want to listen to this shit on her annual day off. Either shut up or piss off home.'

'Steady on there, Jules,' said George.

'Don't you "steady on there" me, you fat ginger bastard. Top up?'

'Aye, go on then. One for the ditch.'

By 2pm, the Atlantic squalls had cleared the land and most of the village folk were happily settled in the Fat Badger. At this time of year, rain stops play and work shuts down. Mid-August, harvest time, building time, painting time. All outdoor jobs. The indoor stuff all saved for winter. Nothing to do now. Only drink.

Because of the storm, no one wanted to leave the pub. The warm Atlantic wind swirled around, whipping up litter and rattling the mouldy guttering, the spew of storm rain hissing against the old single-paned windows of the Fat Badger. Steam rose from the warm slate of Jules's lush beer garden as the raindrops bounced.

The boys sat, gazing out as two, three, then four pints went down. Giant, low-lying blotches of cloud sailed past, bringing thunder that made Jethro's pint glass tremble. Or maybe it was his nerves.

Everyone remained silent, even Frankie, as the epicentre of the storm darkened and shook Little Emlyn.

Jethro was restless; he needed to get out. There was less than a week to go until Lewistock. The worry of all he was about to embark on began to gnaw at him from his insides.

He ducked out of the back door quietly, took his bike and began to cycle towards the coast. Within seconds he was saturated, rain-soaked like he'd not been since he was a kid. It felt soothing. He wondered what his father would think of the rave, now only five days away.

He flew past Roch Castle and accelerated further when he turned onto the St David's road. As he cut faster into the driving rain, he squinted to keep his line. Cars tore past him, jetting long slices of rainwater into his wheels.

As Jethro approached the brow of Newgale hill, he stood up and ground down on the pedals, descending towards the gaping expanse of the bay. He let out a wild, wide-eyed scream, hurtling towards the bubbling sea, a quagmire of foam and funk gurgling to the horizon.

He cycled across the beach road and up onto the cliffs on the south side, then dropped his bike and paced down the footpath towards the edge of the cliff. The gorse slashed across his legs as he went, drawing blood from his numb shins. He felt free, but lost. He was in no man's land. He still didn't know where he'd be this time next week, but he was here, now.

Jethro continued down to the end of a gully that led onto a small drop-off onto the beach used by surfers, sat down on a clump of grass and dangled his feet over the side, breathing deeply.

There were two surfers out among the waves. He watched them for a long moment, like he used to with his mum and dad after school sometimes, when he and Jac had been good. 'OK, run to the beach after tea tonight, boys!' was Trevor's call after the boys had finished their plates on those clear summer evenings. Alone in the rain, the warmth of those memories wasn't enough.

The surfers struggled to paddle out under the huge walls of white water to catch one of the pounding waves. Finally, the blonde surfer succeeded, dropped down the face, legs wide, arms up, in a warrior-charge stance, turned sharply at the bottom with a fluidity that even Jethro knew to appreciate, and tore across the open face of the wave.

As the surfer rode closer to shore, Jethro's mouth dropped open. 'Well fuck me, it's a girl,' he whispered to himself.

At that moment, the wave, twice the height of the girl, sucked up and wrapped in from either side, clapping like small thunder as its angry lips drilled into the shallow water around her. Jethro held his breath. There was nowhere to go. She delicately stepped off the side of the board and the wave came crashing down on her.

She disappeared. Only her board, tombstoning eerily in the ocean spray, was visible.

Jethro stood up.

The girl surfaced. To his surprise, she seemed calm and gently pulled the board towards her using the leg rope. She slid her slender body back onto it, flicked her long blonde hair over the back of her head and took the next wave into shore on her stomach. Wading out of the shallows, she untied her leg rope and wrapped it around the tail of the board and its fins.

Jethro was mesmerised by her form in the wetsuit as she walked straight towards the gully. Slender, feminine, graceful. And with balls of steel.

As she came closer, he could see she was also beautiful. And then he could see she was also familiar. He tried to dry his eyes, but his sleeves were sodden. He blinked his vision clear. It was her.

'Daisy?'

The girl looked up, surprised, and frowned through the thick drizzle. Her eyes widened. 'Jethro?'

'No fucking way. Daisy! My God, what are you doing back here?'

'Ha! I've been back a few months now. Dad got transferred back to the refinery in March. And you? What the hell are you doing sitting there in this weather, you psycho?'

'Long story.'

'Good, I'd love to hear it. Come on, let's go up in the van out of this rain. Got some hot coffee in there. Dad'll be out for a while longer. It's cleaning up out there now, but it's way too heavy for me.'

'You did alright. Fucking hell, that wave you just had was evil. It'd have killed me, hands down.'

'Ah, shut up, you soft cock. It's not that bad.' She waggled her board at Jethro, gesturing him to go in front of her back up the coast path.

'It's good to scare yourself once in a while, don't you think, J?' she asked as they meandered back up the muddy path.

'Ha! Good question. Good timing.'

'What do you mean? You feeling a bit ordinary or something?'

'Er, yes and no.'

'Well, don't be fucking ordinary, Jethro. Life's too short to be a bore.'

Jethro smiled. It was like she hadn't left. He'd always wondered about this day, how they would react to each other after such a long time apart, but he quickly realised she was still the same. That same beautiful, feisty bitch that left him five years ago.

Fate first connected Jethro and Daisy during a game of spin the bottle at the Christmas disco in the school assembly hall, when the bottle brought their lips together.

All was well for three months, until Daisy received the news that her dad was being transferred from Pembroke to an oil refinery in south-west France, and he was taking the family with him. Jethro was devastated, but Daisy took it in her stride and broke off the relationship. 'It's just not going to work, Jethro,' were the words that shattered his delicate fourteen-year-old heart.

They sent postcards to each other for a few months, but that soon fizzled out, and Jethro's wounds slowly healed.

When he received his first blowjob off Meg Morgan in the rugby club changing rooms after Neyland Carnival the following summer, he knew he was going to be alright. But Daisy would always be his first love.

Daisy opened the back door of the campervan and lent Jethro some dry clothes from her dad's box as she squeezed out of her wetsuit. She was like a salt-rubbed Barbie doll, with perfectly toned muscles and the golden skin of an ancient Egyptian princess.

'You're looking good, Dais,' said Jethro as he jigged his brows and smiled wryly, stepping up into the van.

'Cheers, hon. Wish I could say the same about you. You look pooped! Is everything OK?'

'Just get yourself changed and get in here and make that coffee. I'll swing the lamp and get started once I dry off now.'

It took twenty-five minutes for Jethro to tell the story, which gripped Daisy like nothing she'd ever heard before.

'Fucking hell, J, you poor boy. And people like the Growler and Weird Head, they really exist around here?'

Jethro nodded silently.

'That's crazy. And that poor Colwyn. Someone should be strung up for that. Fucking bastards.'

'Aye, you're right.'

'And Mostyn. I'd love to meet him sometime. He sounds amazing.'

'Aye. He's a pretty special bloke. Maybe you can come to the Fat Badger sometime this week for a pint?'

'I'd love to, J,' she said gently.

They held each other's gaze. This was something. No question.

'How was France?' he asked quickly.

'Yeah, good thanks. It's beautiful down there.'

'Where were you again?'

'Place called Bayonne, near Biarritz.'

'Never heard of it.'

'By the sea. Good waves, nice people. My school was nice too.'

'You planning on going back?'

'To live? Nah. It's great to be back in the shire.'

'Got a boyfriend then?' The question shot out of Jethro's mouth like a curveball. He swallowed.

'Uh, kind of.'

Kind of, thought Jethro. He knew what that meant. 'What, he's around here?'

'Yep. He's from town.'

'Who's that then?'

'Dylan Price.'

'Dunno him.'

'You must do, plays rugby for the county and for Narberth.'

'Ah, yeah,' said Jethro. 'The son of Price, the bank manager?'

'Ha. Yep, that's him. He's fucking odd, his old man.'

'Yeah, Mostyn keeps telling me he's a jibbering nutjob.'

They giggled, then fell silent.

Jethro pictured Daisy naked, that spoilt thuggish rugby boy sliding all over her like a reptile, her thin brown legs wrapped around his brutish back. He couldn't stand it. Dylan fucking Price. The twat that wore his collars up, couldn't dance for shit, always stood at the bar with his twat mates with their pints of lager curled into their chests, their puffy oversized arms on display like a mating call for slags. Wankers.

'You've gone quiet, Jethro.'

'Sorry,' said Jethro. He swallowed nervously again, searching for a line. 'Do you know Potts and that lot?'

'Course, we've all been surfing together since we were kids. They were out this morning on the push.'

'What?'

'Sorry, hon, on the incoming tide.'

'Whatever. I need to speak to him. Gotta get that lot to the rave.'

'No worries. Wanna go now?'

'Now?'

'Yep. He lives in Nolton. They'll all be at his place, chillin'. They closed the lifeguard station today, too wild out there. See those red flags?' She pointed across to the centre of the bay. 'They mean bathing's prohibited. They'll just be making the most of the day off. Getting wrecked.'

'Perfect.'

They were dropped outside the house in the early evening. Daisy took her board and wetsuit and told her dad she'd likely stay the night at Potts's and catch an early surf with the boys in the morning. Slippers, the head lifeguard at Newgale, answered the door in his yellow bathrobe and eponymous footwear, and gave the thumbs up to Daisy's dad as he drove off.

As they entered the house, the smell of hashish settled over Jethro like a woolly blanket. They walked down the narrow corridor, following Slippers through the door to the left. The room was black, the curtains fully drawn. Just the flickering lights of the TV illuminated the room like a fading strobe every few seconds.

Jethro counted five boys, lying like casualties, heads tipped sideways. Four were sunken in a circle of comfy chairs, legs sprawled over poufs and tables, with one sleeping in a surfboard bag on the floor behind the sofa.

Daisy had briefed him that these were not just a bunch of young stoners. They were the squad of beach lifeguards entrusted to guard hundreds, even thousands of bathers in the sea at Newgale each summer. They were a couple of years older, but no more wiser or sensible than teenagers. They'd all travelled to Australia on a one-year working holiday visa after dropping out of A levels to join the diaspora of Pembrokeshire surfers living sporadically between Manly and North Narrabeen on the northern beaches of Sydney. In just twelve months they had developed their skills as fearless surfers, as watermen, and honed their talent and capacity for bonging some of the strongest hydroponic weed on the planet.

'Ladies,' said Daisy.

'Alright,' muttered Mole, unable to pull his grinning face away from *Blackadder* on the TV.

'Alright, Dais,' said Potts, more enthusiastic. He turned to look at her. 'Get some waves?'

'Nah, not really,' she said, scrunching up her nose. 'Just a pasting.'

'Ha, me too. Good to get some decent swell though.'

'I hope it's a bit smaller tomorrow.'

'Should be. Should be epic in the morning. Who's your mate?'

'Sorry, this is Jethro, an old friend from school.'

'Hi, Jethro, come on in. You fancy a cone, mate?'

Jethro smiled nervously. 'Hello. Yes, please!'

'Here, boys, shift up a bit and let Jethro squeeze in there.'

The little upheaval of arrangements triggered some groans, but within moments the small bonging den was reorganised, and everyone settled back in for the evening.

Jethro pulled his first bong in one, held it in, and slowly eased back into the sofa. He breathed out, jetting a plume of smoke directly up at the chandelier. Textbook. The boys looked as impressed as was possible through their red piss-hole eyes.

After that one cone, Jethro was stoned. He watched, fascinated, as Mole made his next mull. He toasted four cigarettes while swivelling slowly in his reclining padded office chair. He rotated them in his spindly, magician-like fingers with exemplary timing to ensure all of the white was toasted to a craft-paper brown. He licked the seam of each cigarette like he were playing a tiny harmonica, caressing his lips back and fore with the tops of his nails. He then tore back the sodden seams, opening up their bellies like carcasses, their guts of tobacco falling in clumps into the mixing bowl below. Next was the hash, a lump on the end of pin. Mole flicked the rasping metallic lid off his brass Zippo and lit it up.

He let it burn with a flame for a good few seconds before dropping it into the bowl, immediately working the hash into the tobacco with his fingers. Like butter into flour. He winced with the burn of first contact, but urgency was required. He mixed the mull to an earth-like consistency, the dry-toasted tobacco bonding with the moist and fluffy black hashish.

As the bong went around, they discussed the surf plans for the morning. The lifeguard station had to be set up by 10am, so a dawny, up at 5.30am, was proposed by Potts.

'Fuck off, Potts,' said Oggo, who was comatose in the board bag behind the sofa. 'Six-thirty'll be tidy. Low tide's at five.'

'Yeah, six-thirty should be about right,' agreed Mole.

'Fuck that, boys. This is the first decent swell we've had all summer. It'll be gone tomorrow night. It'll be glass in the morning, no wind, a bit smaller, gangbusters!'

'He's right,' said Daisy, 'corduroy ocean, you pussies. Set your alarms.'

A unified mumble echoed quietly in the room for the five-thirty alarm call.

Jethro stayed quiet. These were the coolest kids he'd ever met. All handsome, with their glossy, sun-soaked eyes, blond straw-like hair and rippling bodies. And they were funny. Piss-takers, talking some strange cult lingo that just rolled off their tongues, like the beach bums in *Home and Away*. He needed them at Lewistock, but he was too stoned to speak. He couldn't even remember the last conversation. He wondered if this is what dementia felt like.

'So what do you do then, Jethro?' asked Potts, out of nowhere. 'I've not seen you around before.'

Jethro tried to piece his mind back together, but the seconds grew more awkward as he realised he'd forgotten what Potts had just asked him.

'He finished in Thommy Pic a while back,' said Daisy. 'He's DJing around at a few clubs and house parties for the summer. And, incidentally, he's organising that rave on Saturday night up in Little Emlyn.'

Slippers surged upright in his chair, reanimated. 'Not Lewistock?' He gaped at Jethro.

'Aye.'

'You're the bloke organising Lewistock?' quizzed Mole in disbelief.

'Yep,' said Jethro.

'Fucking hell. Every cunt is talking about Lewistock!' said Slippers.

'Really?' asked Jethro. 'How did you find out about it?'

'Mate, the whole of North Pembs is buzzing. Everyone's gonna be there. We've been inviting heaps of hot grockle chicks down the beach every day, and they're all mad for it. Hope you don't mind?'

'No, not at all!'

'Tidy. You'd better be ready, son, because there's an army of fucking revellers heading to Little Emlyn on Saturday night, believe you me,' warned Potts.

'Holy fuck.' Jethro bolted up and looked around the room. All the boys sat up, staring at him, like some kind of an attraction. He picked up the bong and packed himself another cone.

The sound of a revving engine woke Jethro. The odour of hovering smoke and bong water almost made him wretch. He pulled himself off the couch quietly, hoping not to wake Daisy. The room was dark, but the sun was rising. He peeked through the curtains and saw an old grey-haired lady, at least in her seventies, in the farmyard across the road. She was wearing green overalls and black wellies and was tying a gate open. She then swung her leg over the seat of the red quad bike parked there, her head thrust backwards as she accelerated off down the road.

'Jesus,' whispered Jethro. He could hardly believe his eyes.

'Old Glenys that is, boy,' whispered a voice that made Jethro jump. 'She's off to fetch the cows. We'd better fuck off before they clog up the road for the next half hour,' said Potts.

Within ten minutes, all seven of them were piled into Potts's two-toned blue-and-white Bedford van, thrashing back the ripe cow parsley on the tight hedges that meandered down the coast road to West Dale.

The van pulled up at the lookout point over the bay and they bundled out from all doors. The conditions were perfect. Blue skies, no wind, swell lines stacked up hundreds of metres out to sea. A solitary surfer, a speck in the bay below, began to paddle quickly out. A set rolled in and Slippers called it.

'Four to five. Easy.'

The surfer caught the second wave of the set, dropped down and slashed fluidly, turn after turn into the wall of blue glass that shimmered across the entire bay.

'That's Tiny Harvatt,' said Daisy.

'Look at him. He surfs like Tom Curren,' said Potts in quiet admiration as Tiny launched off the lip at the end of the closing wave.

'He's as cute as him too,' said Daisy.

'Come on,' said Mole, 'let's just get in there, for fuck's sake.'

'That set was a solid six foot, Slip,' said Daisy, as she observed the size and power of the swell crashing into the headland. 'I think I'll sit this one out till I see you boys getting a few.'

'Buurk bukk bukk bukk,' mocked Oggo, prancing around the van.

'Fuck off, Oggo. Nice to see you finally out of your bong coma and back in the land of the living, you lightweight fucking pussy,' stormed Daisy.

The boys erupted with laughter as they zipped each other's wetsuits up and skipped off down the field towards the beach.

Jethro and Daisy sat together on the headland while the boys picked off the giant rolling waves that peeled perfectly off the left headland of the rugged rocky bay.

'You going in, then?' asked Jethro.

'Nah.'

'Why not? You too ordinary, just like me?'

'Ah, fuck off,' said Daisy, smiling, as she put her head down, her cheeks turning a light shade of red, her hair falling in front of her face.

She slid her hair back over the top of her head, lifted her face and looked into Jethro's eyes. 'You're not ordinary, Jethro Jones. I don't want to go in there because I want to be here with you. I missed you, you know?'

'I missed you too, Daisy Duke.'

They lay back in the long grass, out of view of the boys.

Part III
Chapter 9

The passing of the storm brought a new light to Little Emlyn. The blooming hedges bounced back and the golden barley fields danced in the warm and dry southern winds. Heat returned to the land and the chill of nightfall was forgotten.

Mostyn absorbed himself in the solitude of Lewis Mill, preparing the lanes and mending fences, with just a quiet ensemble of birds and the distant rumble of harvest a tonic for his senses. He felt part of his land, of the soil. He had blossomed and he had withered through the many seasons of his long life, and on this August week in his sixty-fifth year, he felt a calm determination. This was his land, his life, the only thing he could work for, fight for, even die for, because after his days, he knew this land was his only lasting legacy to the Earth.

At 9.20 on Wednesday morning, noise shattered the tranquillity of the farm. Chicken George came tearing through the yard in Mostyn's Land Rover, pulling a horsebox full of equipment, with four burly young farmer recruits on board. Close behind was John the Ghost, clattering along in Mostyn's Massey 135, dragging a red trailer laden with bales of straw, the marquee, a pile of tools and two boys holding tight to the front rack, their bodies jerking into the air with each metallic clack and jolt of the trailer as it bumbled through every puddle well and rock in its path.

As they approached the end of the lane, George stepped off the throttle and slowed to cross the cattle grid. Two of the boys jumped out from behind the tatty cotton siding of the Land Rover and sat on the front bull bars for the mile-long descent through the patchwork of grass and corn stubble fields into the Western Cleddau valley.

After crossing three fields, both vehicles began to descend over the brow that dropped into the bosom of the valley. John's tractor tore past, the boys on the trailer grinning across at George as they rattled and bounced.

George howled with laughter, banging his fist on the top of the steering wheel and nodding his head forward to go faster as he stepped on the pedal and surged ahead. The boys in both vehicles hollered and whooped as they snaked down the grassy bank towards the river at the bottom of the field.

Mostyn was mending a fence around the deep pool and witnessed it all. He heard them from a distance, saw them appearing over the brow, set against the brilliant blue sky. The chase, the challenge, the camaraderie, the laughter. He'd not witnessed so much joy since being a teenager himself and couldn't help but giggle with happiness.

He had only planned to go to the Spar for tobacco, but Biscuits kept walking, marching up through Honeyborough and out onto the main road. He crossed at the roundabout and headed into the countryside towards Rosemarket.

His father was alive, but Biscuits felt neither joy nor relief as he strode along the quiet road. He dragged his right hand pensively across the faces of the cow parsley that spilled from the hedgerow as he pondered his new darkness.

He climbed over a broken rusty gate and walked across a grass field into a wooded area, hidden from the road in a small river valley. He sat on a fallen tree and rolled a cigarette, looking at the woods all around him as he exhaled quietly, jigging his knees with anxiety. As the minutes passed, nature's silence crept quickly over him. His inferiority in the world sank in and he felt humbled, but not hopeful.

A cloud drifted across the sun's path. Shadow swamped the wood. The image of his father lying in a hospital bed, bandages holding together his broken skull, filled Biscuits' mind. Dean was still not yet conscious, but he was stable, out of his coma. Biscuits did not know how he would ever look his father in the eyes again. He didn't want to say sorry. He didn't want to make amends. He hated him more than ever, for pushing him, pushing him over the edge. He never asked for it, he never provoked it. Attacked for riding in the car of the nicest man he'd ever met. A man who'd shown more interest in him in one day than his father had in his entire lifetime.

Now, here he was. Everyone would find out. His father's wounds would heal in time, but Biscuits would always carry the vivid mark of the betrayer. He knew his father would make sure of that.

He wished he had killed him.

Jethro, Boutros and Daisy continued distributing the flyers, and by Friday afternoon Jethro was satisfied that the job was done. The Radio I Roadshow drew the youth of the entire county, north and south, and Jethro was bewildered by the number of enthusiastic strangers that approached him for information and directions to Lewistock.

Despite the excitement in Tenby and Saundersfoot, Jethro could not stop worrying about Biscuits. He had heard that Dean's skull was smashed up and that he was in hospital, but nothing more. The fact that Biscuits had literally vanished since the day in Tenby made Jethro fear the worst. He had witnessed Biscuits' dark side on a few occasions in the past when his father was home, knew that one day things would come to blows. But he hadn't imagined this.

Boutros treated Jethro and Daisy to lunch in the Plantagenet, Tenby's oldest restaurant. They sat in the hearth of its giant Flemish chimney and went through the list of jobs still to be done. Lewistock was only thirty-six hours away.

'Shit,' said Daisy as she put her head down and looked again at the menu.

Jethro frowned at Boutros, then looked around.

'Daisy?'

Daisy looked up and forced a smile, tucking her hair behind her left ear. 'Hi.'

'I thought it was you. What are you doing down here?' asked Rosemary Price, Dylan's mother, looking curiously at Jethro and Boutros.

'Just down for the Roadshow with my old school friend Jethro here and his granddad.'

Boutros raised his eyebrows.

'I see. Dylan is around somewhere. I'm meeting him outside Tenby House in about ten minutes. I'll tell him you're here.'

'Great,' said Daisy.

Rosemary left and Daisy dropped her head onto the table.

'It's not that bad, Dais. It's just your boyfriend,' said Jethro, grinning.

'Yeah, but I told him I was helping my gran today. He asked me to come down to the Roadshow with him.'

'Ooops.'

'Yep, he's gonna be raging.'

'Don't worry,' said Boutros reassuringly.

Minutes later, Dylan Price entered the restaurant with two friends, the three of them dressed in shell suits and rugby shirts, like they'd just come from training.

'He's here!' whispered Jethro excitedly. He'd been watching the door like a hawk since Rosemary left.

Jethro observed Boutros watching the three lads, with increased bewilderment, as they strutted across the restaurant floor. Chests out, fists clenched and all three looking like they were carrying invisible TVs under both arms.

'Dear God,' muttered Boutros.

'Alright. I thought you was helping your gran clean the cottage today?' said Dylan.

'I was, but Jethro called me last minute to come down.'

Jethro raised his head and smiled humbly at Dylan.

'Sorry, but who the fuck are you, Jethro? I've never heard of you before.' Dylan breathed in and expanded his chest further.

'Calm down, Dylan. Jethro's an old friend of mine from Thommy Pic. We used to hang out before I went to France. We just bumped into each other down Newgale last week.'

'Well isn't that a lovely story, Daisy. Why did you fucking lie to me about today?'

'I didn't lie to you, Dyl. It was just a spontaneous thing this morning, seriously,' said Daisy, calm and sincere.

Dylan looked at her and his anger seemed to dissipate. 'And what's this?' He pulled out a Lewistock flyer from his shell suit pocket. 'You gave this to one of the boys about an hour ago,' he said, wagging his finger at Jethro.

Jethro was shocked he'd given a flyer to someone dressed like that. 'Don't you remember?'

'Not really. We've given out hundreds here this week,' said Jethro.

'So is this your party?'

'Yep.'

'So, open invitation, yeah? I can bring all the boys?'

Oh fucking hell, Jethro thought to himself. 'Yeah, yeah, no worries.'

'Tidy. It's not going to be just full of fucking pillheads now, is it?'

'It's a rave,' said Jethro, 'but no, there's a bar there as well. There'll be all sorts and geezers there.'

Dylan screwed up his face. 'Whatever. We might pop up. See how it's looking in town first.'

'Awesome,' said Jethro.

'I'll see you tonight, yeah, Dais?'

'Yeah. I'll drop round on the way home, around five, six, OK?'

'Tidy.'

Dylan stepped over to kiss Daisy. She raised her face up to him and smiled as their lips met; Jethro had a ringside seat. What the fuck was she doing with that prick?

Dylan winked victoriously at Jethro as he strutted off.

There was silence until Boutros broke the ice. 'He's quite different from you, if you don't mind me saying, Daisy.'

'I know, but he's alright. He looks after me. I should have told him about today. I'm not surprised he's pissed off.'

'He's a fucking twat,' said Jethro.

'You don't even know him!' said Daisy. 'He's just driven to succeed, one of those types.'

'But look at the cunt. He wears a fucking shell suit and a rugby shirt to the Radio 1 fucking Roadshow! You're honestly proud to be his girlfriend? Jesus Christ, I just don't get it.'

Daisy's face dropped. 'OK. If you really want to get it, Jethro, he's good in bed and he's got a massive cock.' She grinned at him. 'Get it now?'

Boutros ordered the bill and they left.

Jethro was in the middle of measuring his penis when the phone rang.

'Fuck.' He grabbed a towel and ran downstairs, dropping the ruler back in the mail tray. He picked up the phone. It was Daisy.

'Sorry, J, you were right. He's a bellend. I just went over to his house and he just exploded, gave me loads of shit about you, called me a slag, saying he'd never tolerate any bitch humiliating him like that. Ryan, that fat fuck with him today, recognised you and remembered we were together before.'

'Did you finish with him?'

'No, I just stormed out. But I will, I promise. I just need to go back over there. I've got my best board in his garage. I'll do it then. Jesus. He's such a fucking tool.'

'Told you so.'

'I know. Sorry, J. I just have this instinct to always stick up for those closest to me, and he was one of those up until about an hour ago. I knew all along he wasn't really my type, but you know how we have to go on that journey and try different things to find what we truly want.'

'Like a big cock?'

'J! No! It wasn't that big anyway. I just said that to piss you off.'

'Hmmm...'

'What are you up to? Measuring your cock?'

'Ha! Yeah, yeah, I've got a big plastic metre jutting out of my pants as we speak. Need to find a second one I think.'

'You're funny. Can I come to the pub with you tonight, sexy boy?'

'Suppose so.'

The Fat Badger was like a war room, its soldiers on the cusp of the final push. The beers flowed as lists were checked and the spirit of Lewistock began to take hold.

All evening, Mowbray Codd sat on his own under the stuffed badgers, his head rotating like a barn owl's, its senses under assault, absorbing the artillery of life taking place all around him through his thick, foggy brown spectacles.

Boutros had briefed Mostyn on Mowbray's odd behaviour in the vestry and Mostyn had not had the chance to speak to him since. As a long-serving mason, Mowbray had the power to destroy Lewistock with one phone call.

Mostyn tightened his tie and took a deep breath. 'Mind if I join you, Mo?'

Mowbray was startled and frowned up at Mostyn. 'Please.' He extended his bloated arm to welcome Mostyn to the table.

'You alright, boy? You look a bit detached there, if you don't mind me saying. Is everything OK?'

Mowbray smiled. 'Aye, I'm alright.'

'Sure?'

Mowbray was quiet for a long moment. 'Do you know, Mostyn, I've watched you all your life, battling through the storms. First Gareth. Then your ma and pa. You've been drenched in your oilskins and covered in shit, for what? Fifty years now?'

Mostyn was taken aback and sniggered shyly. 'Aye, summat like that.'

'But you've lived, Mostyn. Look at you. I can't imagine the dark days you've endured alone in Lewis Mill, but I've also seen you on those glorious days. That darkness, it nourished you. You've always bounced back. I respect that.'

Mostyn looked at the floor sternly, blinking, unsure how to respond. He leaned in closer to the table and spoke quietly. 'I guess, Mo, over time, even though your body and mind can be ripped to shreds, the human spirit remains unbreakable.' He paused. 'If you can weather the storm, your spirit will get stronger, more resilient. That's for sure. You can choose to sit in sadness, paralysed, or you can choose to grow strength, and treasure the most precious gift of all – life itself. After Gareth, I always chose life, and spirit – for him, mostly. I've never stopped missing him. Every day.' Mostyn paused again in the memory, then looked up at Mowbray. 'Nothing on God's Earth is as resilient as the human spirit. I firmly believe that, Mo.'

Mowbray tried to smile, but his eyes betrayed him. 'I'm not sure,

Most. Look at me. Sat in that Post Office for forty-five bloody years. I just existed. Sometimes I wonder if I was even born with any spirit. I've never left the shore. My entire life has just morphed into one long boring Goddamn day. An overcast one. No downpours, but no rose-tinted sunshine either. Life has just passed me by.'

'Come on now, boy,' said Mostyn, 'you can't say that. We've had some wonderful t—'

'Aye, we did, but those were all in another lifetime to me now. But look at you, you're still living, riding on the high seas.'

'Aye, still getting bloody battered, wave after wave!'

'You should be proud of what you've achieved with this Lewistock, Mostyn. I haven't seen the community so alive and together like this in twenty-odd years. What you are doing tomorrow is right for that very reason.'

'Thank you, Mo, but we've got to pull it off first, old pal. We still have it all to do.'

'You'll be fine, Mostyn. I have no doubt.'

They held each other's eyes for a moment. Mowbray stood up to leave.

'See you tomorrow night then, Mo?' shouted Mostyn with a smile, just before Mowbray went out of sight.

'Oh, aye!' shouted Mowbray, but Mostyn was unsure what that meant.

At 1am, Jethro called time. There were exactly twenty-four hours to go until the lights went on in the Tenby nightclubs and the convoys of ravers began their journey through the Pembrokeshire countryside to Lewistock.

Mostyn and Jethro walked back to Lewis Mill together and neither spoke a word.

It was a beautiful morning, dampened only by Mostyn's sighting of a solitary magpie hopping about on his lawn.

By teatime, the Lewistock site was teeming with farmers, children and the entire WI, all drinking cider and scoffing sausage rolls and scones. Two pale skinny roadies wearing black Marshall Amplification T-shirts made eyes at each other as Joyce danced around them during the soundcheck, flashing her knickers at the red-headed one. He looked aroused and disgusted in equal measure, quickly burying his blushing face behind the speakers.

The straw bales, strewn in a circle out in the sunshine, were covered with farmhands and village ladies cackling like long-lost hens in the burning afternoon heat. Just like the good old days, thought Mostyn, the grey hairs standing on end on his thick, muscular forearms.

'What the fuck are they doing?' asked Jethro, pointing at two old ladies putting up a table next to the entrance of the marquee.

'Putting up a cake stand. They reckon they'll make over three hundred quid if they sell the lot. Haven't you seen all the cakes in the back of Joyce's car?'

'Please tell me you're fucking kidding me, Most?'

'What now? What's wrong with that? They've been baking all bloody week for us, you ungrateful little shit.'

'Alright, alright, calm down.' Jethro sighed and placed his hands on Mostyn's shoulders. 'I hope you're ready for tonight, old man,' he said gently. 'Please keep an open mind about everyone who turns up and let's make sure we stick to the game plan, yeah? A tenner each. No blaggers. Not fucking one. It clearly says on the flyer, everyone knows. Make sure Frankie is on it, OK?'

'Aye, aye. John is with him as well. We'll be fine.'

'Right, we gotta go,' said Jethro. Cars of local revellers were filing up the valley side. 'Wish me luck! I'll see you later. You should see the car lights coming down the valley from around half one.'

'Good luck, son. Everything is going to be alright. You go get us some ravers.' Mostyn gave two thumbs up and a smile as George's yellow van pulled off and chugged its way slowly back up the valley, directly into the path of the big afternoon sun.

Then it hit Mostyn. There was no going back. He felt the veins slowly contracting all over his body, felt his deep heartbeat as the yellow van became smaller and smaller. He took deep breaths to settle himself as he stood there, alone.

Mostyn felt a tug on the fabric behind his knee. He turned.

'Hiya, Ted. What you up to, boy?'

'Nothing, just playing. What's a rave, Mr Thomas?'

Mostyn huffed with amusement. 'That's a very good question, Ted. I'm not too sure I know the answer to that myself.'

'Well, that's a bit weird. Daddy said you were having one here tonight.'

'That's right, Ted. That's why we have this lovely marquee here and a bar for drinks. Nice, isn't it?'

'Mummy said we can't stay long because there will be lots of crazy people everywhere later.'

'Oh, did she now? That's lovely. Well, it's a good job your daddy's here to help me keep an eye on all of these crazy people then, isn't it?'

'Oh, he's definitely not staying. He's more scared than Mummy about the crazy people.'

Mostyn patted Ted on the head and looked back up the valley side — the cars had gone, just a haze of old diesel fumes and dust dissipating into the bright sun.

The yellow van passed Chequers nightclub at 7pm and activity outside was already brewing. In Tenby, families still trooped up from the beaches as swathes of waifish golden-skinned young clubbers poured into the pubs. The heat of the day continued into the evening, energising them with a warm aura of promiscuity as they dropped half tablets of ecstasy with their pints and the night began to take hold.

A symphony of whistles went off in the Night Owl as Jon of the Pleased Wimmin stepped up to join Danny Slade in the DJ booth for the final set. Jon wore a black sequin dress, short and tight, twinkling like galaxies against the flashing lights. His hair was long and straight, perfectly groomed, peroxide blond, drawn across one eye like a sultry whore. His face, delicate as a porcelain doll's, was finished with bright red lipstick and fuck-me eyelashes.

Jethro gazed at him longingly, almost forgetting himself, glided gently towards him through the crowd and handed him a flyer. Jon frowned at the piece of paper as he read it, then cast it dramatically up into the air. He winked at Jethro and turned and opened his record box.

Jethro smiled in defeat. He didn't really care. He felt sublime, the warm peaceful waves of ecstasy lapping through him. He wondered why he could never remember the feeling, always content in his introspections, where everything made sense. He thought of Daisy, of Lewistock and of Mostyn. He looked at the faces across the dance floor and felt the moment. The most perfect moment in the most perfect day of his life. He wanted to keep the feeling forever, but knew that was the magic – he could never take it with him.

A hand pulled on his shoulder. A voice yelled, 'At least you fucking tried, J.' Jethro turned around. It was Biscuits, smiling, eyes sloshing, huffing his cheeks as the rushes pinged through him. They rocked each other like long-lost brothers.

Even before the lights came on, clubbers began to float down the grand staircase of the club, the word Lewistock seeping from their lips like a secret curse. Outside, beats thumped and ravers danced, music flowing through their limbs like wind through an air sock. As the crowds poured out, the car park swelled and the warm sea air crackled with the sounds of hedonistic youth at the height of its power.

Biscuits and Sparky cascaded down the stairs and out through the doors, their floppy arms thrown over each other's shoulders as they staggered into the car park like two space monkeys in a three-legged race.

'Fucking hell, boys,' said Potts, dazzled by their eyes and Biscuits' frantic gnawing at his lower lip. 'You alright?'

Sparky fell forward into Potts's arms, giggling like a madman, whispering into his ear, 'Microdots.'

'You haven't?'

They had.

Potts headed towards Jethro and Daisy, who were drifting around the car park, trying to start the convoy with Gurnard as the lead driver.

'You sure you want Gurnard in front?' asked Daisy.

'Yeah, yeah,' said Jethro.

'You sure? Look at him.'

Gurnard's mouth was clasped around the top of the steering wheel, his top lip drawn back, his teeth exposed, his eyes glaring ahead as his head bobbed quickly to the happy hardcore blaring from the tinny speakers of his van.

'He looks like a mad dog,' said Daisy.

'Aye,' said Jethro. 'He'll be fine.'

'Jethro, keep an eye on those two space cadets. They've banged acid,' said Potts, pointing at Biscuits and Sparky as they piled into the back of Gurnard's van.

'Jesus,' said Jethro, but his train of thought was derailed when he spotted a Gamorrean guard in a tuxedo at the nightclub door, only fifty yards away.

Potts glared into the van at Gurnard and shook his head at the state of him. Even with the overwhelming waves of affection pumping through Potts's veins, he still wanted to punch Gurnard in the face for violating his mother.

By the time George's van reached Canaston Bowl, scores of cars were already backed up in both directions towards both Templeton and Carew.

Jethro stepped out of the van, passed the bong back to Daisy, blew a cloud of sweet smoke up into the empty sky and climbed up onto the roof, absorbing the warm sea of lights. The convoys morphed into sparkling carnival flotillas, sailing on tar canals under stars so bright they almost made the black sky disappear.

'Get on with it!' screamed a big black lady in a bright Caribbean dress with a bunch of bananas on her head. She was driving a London cab. Her flabby naked arm banged furiously on the outside of the cab door. 'Get on with it! Get on with it!'

Jethro jumped down, scared, and looked back at her, but she wasn't there.

As the cars began their journey through the lanes, Jethro studied the glow of the convoys, tailing for miles, illuminated in the sea mist. Though his vision was blurred, his eyes were drawn to the riders in the car behind. He couldn't focus on them, but he could sense they didn't fit. He squinted and their ghostly faces finally came together. 'Oh, no.' He stayed calm. He squeezed Daisy's arm softly, turned to her and spoke quietly into her ear, 'Can you see who's behind, Dais?'

Daisy leaned forward and looked out of the window.

Weird Head blew her a kiss.

She slammed her head back against the panel.

'It's them, isn't it?' whispered Daisy.

'Yes. Fuck 'em.' Jethro put his head down and began to roll a joint. Streams of ants marched out of the shadows, all over his hands.

Chapter 10

By the time Mostyn had lit the bonfire, many of the villagers had gone. Joyce and Mary were still fussing over their cake stand, doing their best to look sober. Only Eddie Taurus, the local superstar DJ, remained in the marquee, practising his opening set, while the usual suspects were getting rowdy in the bar, arm-wrestling Frankie and telling increasingly tall tales.

The bonfire roared, the flames spreading so quickly that within minutes they were licking the drooping branches of the old oak tree nearby, just metres overhead. Mostyn moved and knocked the pallets off the top of the burning pile with his pitchfork. The flames settled.

Ruth came out of the beer tent and stood next to Mostyn. He sensed her there. They watched the flames without saying a word.

Of all the people hitching to the rave, Gurnard stopped for the shaman and the witch.

'Check out these cunts,' said Deri. Gurnard swerved to avoid a thumb protruding from a wizard's sleeve.

'Pick them up!'

Gurnard pulled over and Deri wound down the window. The man was quite young, early twenties, had long, shaggy brown hair, an unkempt goatee beard and was covered in a black velvet cloak with purple lining. The woman beamed them a smile, similar aged and wearing a white cotton dress, a chain of flowers around her flowing red hair

'Lewistock?' asked Deri.

'Yes, if you have space,' said the man, 'that would be great.'

The cars behind began to toot as the convoy ground to a halt.

'No worries. Quick, hop in the back.'

The man and woman opened the back door and climbed in. Biscuits and Sparky froze, confused, checking one another's reactions.

'Hello there, I'm Soren, and this is Sayer,' he said.

'Alright,' said Sparky.

'Alright. I'm Biscuits, and that's Sparky.' Biscuits felt his mouth tremble as he spoke from the shadows.

Sayer kept smiling at them, observing discreetly for some minutes as their jawbones looked to her like they were trying to knead their way out of their skins. 'Are you OK, boys?' she said quietly.

'Off my head. Fuckin' flying,' said Biscuits, his mouth cupping out small puffs of air and his hands rubbing anxiously against his knees.

'Well, I'm not OK,' huffed Sparky, patting his head quickly with both hands. 'I'm off my fucking tits. Are you really dressed like a wizard?'

Soren smiled. 'Yes. Don't worry,' he said calmly. 'I'm actually a shaman, not a wizard.'

'Fucking hell, you trying to spin me out?'

'No, no, not at all.' Soren put his hand up and pulled back from the boys, their unpredictable kaleidoscopic eyes unnerving him. 'I'm sorry if you think that.'

Conversation in the back of the van fell silent, and only the sounds of Gurnard's happy hardcore rattled through the cloudy plastic window.

The van turned off the tarmac and bounced along Lewis Mill lane. Biscuits and Sparky began to slide deeper into their trips, faces pinched, eyes dancing.

Soren turned to Sayer, whispering.

'What the fuck's going on, Biscuits?' asked Sparky in a panic.

'Hey, hey, it's OK,' said Sayer softly. She placed her warm hand on Sparky's knee. 'We were just hitching to Lewistock and your kind friends in the front there stopped to pick us up. We didn't just appear. We're here for a good time, just like you.'

The paranoia wouldn't leave Biscuits. 'You don't look like ravers.'

'We're not,' said Soren. 'Like I said, I'm a shaman and Sayer is a white witch, but not like you imagine from the fairy stories. We're just practising healers, that's all.'

'What, like doctors?' asked Biscuits.

'Exactly, except we channel transcendental energies from the spirit world to heal people, instead of using conventional Western medicine.'

The boys' faces gaped at Soren. He really did look like a wizard.

'How do you channel energies from the spirit world?' quizzed Sparky. He was awestruck.

'We seek an altered state of consciousness where we can place one foot in the spirit world and one foot right here on Earth.'

'Wow.' Sparky shook his head.

Biscuits thought hard for a moment. Finally he spoke. 'Do you want to buy some acid?'

'Erm, sure! That would be great,' said Soren.

'Microdots. Fiver a piece. Tidy.'

'Great, we'll take one, then—'

'Two,' Sayer butted in, still smiling like a horse.

'Lights!' yelled Frankie. He dashed to pick up his Quality Street tin from behind the beer taps. The bar went silent and the village folk slowly stepped out of the tent and looked up at the brow of the valley. Eddie Taurus glanced up from the decks and saw the wonder on their faces. He stopped the music. Silence swamped the plain as the convoy of lights glowed like a white vain spilling over the horizon, seeping down into the blackness of the valley, edging closer. The distant thuds of bass advanced like muffled war drums. The villagers watched like castaways, mesmerised, as modern life forms descended upon them to save or to destroy their secret little world.

Eddie smiled and rubbed his hands quickly together with excitement. He hopped back onto the stage and carefully dropped the stylus onto the record. As it spun, the crackle of the vinyl fizzed like a firecracker through the humming speakers and the bass began to thump.

Within twenty minutes, the Quality Street tin was full. Frankie began stuffing notes into his pockets as the cars flooded the valley, but vehicles began to overtake the queue on the last stretch down onto the plain. Within minutes, the slow but orderly convoy came to a grinding halt. A bottleneck had swelled like a balloon in the last gateway that led down to Lewistock. Horns blared, people shouted, doors slammed, but quickly cars were abandoned, doors left open as the ravers burst out of them. Cats out of cages. Lewistock, in full-view just a few hundred yards below them, twinkled and throbbed, seducing them to bound down the dusty lane into the wall of crisp electronic sound.

Many tried to avoid Frankie and John the Ghost on the gate, diverting into the woods, filtering through the dark trees, pouring into the field.

Within five minutes of stepping out of Gurnard's van, Biscuits and Sparky had lost each other. Deri tried to keep them all together, but soon gave up.

'What you doing down there, Biscuits?' asked Daisy, who'd spotted him on the fringe of the hedge. He was alone, lying on his back, smoking a joint, gazing up into the universe.

'I'm having a lovely time.'

'Come on, let's get in there!'

She scooped him up from the ground and they both staggered into the marquee. His face lit up as he reconnected with the night. He shuffled back into a corner in front of a speaker, closed his eyes and began to throw his head to the beat.

Jethro was up on the stage with Eddie when he spotted Mostyn through the back of the marquee, putting petrol into the generator. Looking at the old man, in his suit, wellies and flat cap, made him tingle. Jethro was caressed away into a parallel space. He watched bodies popping to the same rhythm, each in their own magical way. Uninhibited movements, interconnected, sealed with smiles.

He looked up into the sky and closed his eyes. 'I miss you, Dad,' he whispered and the beats seemed to throb through his ribcage. When he opened his eyes, Mostyn was looking straight at him, the petrol can still in his hand. Jethro smiled and gave a lazy salute. Mostyn smiled back and returned a thumbs-up before turning and disappearing behind the tent.

Jethro looked across into the packed beer tent, the striplights above the bar lighting the area with a surreal glow. Steam was rising visibly from the crowds. He could see Frankie arm-wrestling with some rugby boys, but Dylan Price wasn't one of them. Jethro chuckled at Frankie's animated face. His mouth motoring, the boys nodding intently, Frankie's words of wisdom pouring out like shit from a slurry tanker as he rolled the sleeves even higher up his arms.

Jethro saw Joyce. She was steaming, walking sideways while chewing the ears off Mostyn's new neighbours, Giles and Imogen. They both beamed and nodded with a look of polite horror as they courteously ate the slices of chocolate cake she had given them.

Ruth was sitting at the bar, talking and laughing with Boutros. Jethro thought she looked lovely. A kind face, but with some of the similar signs of sadness that reminded Jethro of his mum. He immediately blocked the train of thought and his eyes settled on Chicken George, who was going for gold with a group of horny-looking horsey girls. Way out of his depth. His green Global Hypercolor T-shirt had turned yellow all around his armpits and down his back. One of the girls noticed and made a vomiting gesture to her friend. Jethro smirked.

Something else caught his eye. He turned his head and there was Dylan Price and one of his meathead friends, topless on the bass bins, their faces twisting like they were chewing angry wasps.

'Look at those clowns,' shouted Potts into Jethro's ear. Jethro came to and burst out laughing. They chuckled like small kids.

'They've been looking for pills all night. Their first time apparently,' said Potts.

'No shit,' said Jethro as he smiled, passed his joint to Potts and began to dance.

Jethro felt a tap on his shoulder. John the Ghost and Chicken George were beckoning him urgently out of the tent, back towards the gate. Boutros was speaking diplomatically to two men dressed like they'd just arrived at the wrong party. They hadn't. They were the licensing officers from the county council, and Frankie had just tried to charge them ten pounds each for entry.

Frankie was sitting on a nearby rock, cursing himself.

'Where's Mostyn?' asked Jethro. 'Where the fuck is he?'

'He just took off in his Land Rover,' said George. 'He must have shit the bed and legged it.'

'He wouldn't do that,' said John the Ghost, his eyes watching the brow of the valley.

For decades, in some of the poorest countries on Earth, Boutros had negotiated with despots, gangsters, crooks and chancers, but it was clear that the two officers from Pembrokeshire County Council were having none of it. As one filled in a report form, the other made his way back to the unmarked car to CB a call back to Haverfordwest police station for a team to shut down the rave. He picked up the CB handle and clicked the button, silencing the distorted hiss as his lips neared the mouthpiece.

'Wait,' shouted John. 'Look, that must be the police coming down now. I just spoke to an undercover officer in the marquee and he said he's made the call.'

Both officers frowned, but they seemed intrigued by a solitary set of lights making its way down the dark valley side. They were all silent as the lights approached. John heard the diesel engine before it came into view and prayed Mostyn was about to pull something miraculous out of the hat.

The doors opened and out of the Land Rover stepped Mostyn and Mowbray Codd. Mowbray was wearing a navy satin dressing gown, stripy brown pyjamas and sheepskin slippers.

'Dear God,' said Boutros as he turned to Jethro, John and George, 'we're buggered now, gents.'

'Evening all,' said Mostyn, perkily, as the group stood frozen.

'Hello, officers. I'm Mostyn Thomas. This is my land.' He reached out and shook both officers' hands firmly. 'Could we have a word in private please, with Mr Codd here?' Mostyn waved them forward to join him and Mowbray. The officer filling in the report tried to speak, but the sight of Mowbray in his bedclothes left him stammering. He was quiet as they wandered back up the dark lane.

They began to talk. Within seconds, the discussion had become heated.

Three minutes later, the men all shook hands, turned and walked back down to the gate. The officers branched off at their unmarked car, opened the doors and stepped inside.

Mostyn winked at Jethro, struggling to conceal his smugness. Jethro's face lit up as the car pulled away. 'It's on like Donkey Kong, boys!' he shouted, reaching his arms across and embracing Mowbray affectionately. Mowbray was visibly shocked, but obviously touched. He broke out in a wide smile not witnessed on his face for months, maybe years.

'Come on, Frankie,' said Boutros, 'stop crying, you big baby. It's alright, the show goes on!'

Sparky had wandered off. He followed the treeline up the valley in search of something but forgot what that something was. There was a figure in the middle of the dark field. A scarecrow, maybe, but as he crept towards it, he saw it move. It was a man. He was only twenty yards away when Sparky shouted over to him. 'Hey!'

Soren span around, his eyes sparkling like the devil's.

'What you doing, man?' asked Sparky.

'This is it! This is it!' said Soren, excited.

'This is what?'

'The Valley of Grief!'

'What d'you mean?'

'*The Mabinogion*, it's wrong! I knew it! Ha!' He lowered his voice and looked narrowly at Sparky. 'A few months ago, I had a vision that the Valley of Grief was right here, on the banks of the Cleddau. It's taken me weeks to find it, but this is it! I knew all along it was never in the north!'

As Sparky stared at the shaman, Soren's face began to simmer, then bubble. His nose grew like Pinocchio's and his chin grew longer and longer until his long floppy nose came to rest on it, ten inches away from his face. The chin and nose morphed into a beak. Soren was turning into a crow. Feathers were appearing on his cape as his face went completely black and his yellow eyes bore deep into Sparky's.

Sparky felt the wind pick up. The trees around them began to sway and hiss.

'Something bad will happen tonight,' whispered Soren. 'It's in the cards! The cards!' he yelled.

Sparky closed his eyes and slapped his face over and over again. He opened them – Soren's face had returned to normal.

'Shut the fuck up, you freak. You're fucking spinning me out, OK?' said Sparky.

'The Coraniaids. Watch out for the Coraniaids. They're here!'

'What are they?'

'Woodland dwarves. They're there, in *The Mabinogion*.'

'What the fuck is that?'

'The book. The book!'

'You're off your fucking head.' Sparky turned and began to pace back towards the music. He felt the grass growing under his feet as he walked, green blades surging up, twisting, trying to wrap around his ankles. He kicked them off.

'Don't speak badly of the Coraniaids. They will hear you! They hear everything!' shouted Soren.

'Fuckin' shut up and leave me alone.'

Soren began to follow him. 'They hear every word the wind touches. You can't kill them!'

'FUCK OFF!'

'Hear the whispers in those trees? That's them! That's them! They've heard us!'

Sparky heard the whispers immediately.

'Maaaark, Maaaark,' they repeated. 'Maaaark, Maaaark.'

'How the fuck do they know my name?' he whimpered, looking all around him. The whispers got louder, swirling and hissing from all areas of the valley. He closed his eyes and ran as fast as he could across the field back towards Lewistock.

'Hey!' yelled a gruff voice.

Sparky stopped running and looked across. There was an oldish man, nasty-looking, standing under a tree, skinny, dressed in black, bald and full of wrinkles. It was Ronnie. Sitting next to him was a large young man, not more than twenty-five. He looked like a thug, with a tattoo of the Neyland fern down the left side of his neck, his head in his hands. He was coughing and retching.

'You looking for pills, son?'

Sparky didn't know what he was looking for, but he thought a pill could level him out, tame the acid, dampen the hallucinations. He had to do something. 'Yeah, OK. How much are they?'

'Free to a good home, son. Here you go.' Ronnie tossed the bag of blue tablets at Sparky, who only saw the glittering trail of the bag as it fell to the ground. He bent down, picked up the bag and put it in his pocket without looking at its contents. He turned to Ronnie, said thank you and staggered across the field, navigating through clouds of marijuana smoke and bodies strewn across the grass.

'What the fuck did you do that for, Ron?' asked the other man.

'What?'

'Give that kid those pills. I only took a quarter. It's fucking poisoned me.' The thug continued to cough, speckles of blood spraying onto his hand, his head pounding.

'Shut up, Sludge. You're soft as shit.'

'What the fuck's going on?' asked Jethro, as the tractor approached the marquee and people began to panic. He forced his way through the crowds and out into the field. The tractor's lights were on full beam and blinding. It stopped, the door was flung open and, in slow motion, a woman stepped out. A stunner, long, straight blonde hair, succulent cherry lips, dressed in a tight black sequin dress. Jethro moved forward and started running towards her. 'No way. No fucking way!'

It was Jon of the Pleased Wimmin.

Jethro extended his hand to help Jon off the last step of the tractor.

'I can't believe it! Thanks so much for coming. I'm Jethro.'

'Hiya, love. Well my name was on the flyer, Jethro. I don't like to disappoint. I'll just be sending you the dry-cleaning bill for all this fucking cowshit, yeah?' Jon winked. 'Wow, this does look like a party, Jethro.'

Behind Jon in the cab was Mostyn at the wheel, exchanging banter with Danny Slade.

'I found these two lost on the lane there,' shouted Mostyn.

Danny passed the record boxes down as the word buzzed around at light-speed. Crowds swarmed out of the tents, gathering in disbelief around the glow of the tractor, an otherworldly mirage in this otherworldly place. Jon smiled and waved playfully around at the crowds, like the Queen.

Frankie appeared from nowhere and offered Jon his hand. 'May I?' he said tenderly.

'Ooof, the days of chivalry are not lost on you, are they, big boy?' Jon smiled and took Frankie's hand. Frankie blushed and led their guest across the field and into the marquee.

Jethro smiled up at Mostyn.

'Have fun now, son,' he said. 'That's enough action for me for one night. I'm off to bed.' He heaved the tractor door closed and disappeared, bouncing his way up the lane.

Jethro blew him a kiss as he vanished out of sight.

Jon Pleased and Danny Slade stepped up to join Eddie Taurus on stage and a roar went up in the marquee.

'Hiya, Steve,' said Slippers.

'Hey, man,' said Steve, staggering past with a staff in his hand, a branch from a nearby oak tree.

'Who's Steve?' asked Biscuits as he passed the joint back to Slippers.

'Him.'

'No, it's not. That's Soren, the shaman.'

'No, it's not. That's Steve, from Telford.'

'What?'

'Yeah, I studied with him last year.'

'What, that shamanism shit?'

'No, computer science, BTEC, in the college of knowledge.'

'He told me he was a shaman.'

'Well he's not. He's a knob.'

'Fuck off?'

'Prize fucking prick. He turned up at the freshers' party last year in a *Dungeons & Dragons* T-shirt. He was always reading comics and weird wizard shit. Then I heard he got into the mushrooms. Is he tripping now?'

'Yeah. I sold him a microdot.'

'Aye, well, there we go then.'

They both watched, astonished, as Soren lifted his staff into the air with both hands. He was illuminated by the light of the bonfire, staring down at the ground.

'By the power of fucking Grayskull,' muttered Biscuits.

Sparky's eyes opened, jarred by a crushing pain in his head. The acrid chemical taste in his mouth made him gag. He tried and failed to draw saliva to spit the bitterness away, gazing unsteadily around him.

He was in a forest.

His vision was mottled with a hazy network of grids, a net of dayglow fibres cast in tiny squares. On the other side was a distorted world.

He looked down. In his hand, a moneybag, half full of blue tablets. Some had fallen onto the floor. His head continued to throb. He was completely lost.

The forest began to breathe and gurgle and the whispers came again. They started from a distance, flitting towards him, then whooshing closer, high in the trees, from under the shrubs, moving nearer. 'Maaaark, Maaaark,' they purred. His head swivelled and spun, trying to connect. 'Sssparky, Ssssparky...'

An odd-shaped tree stump caught his eye. He stared at it for a long moment and it began to warp into a figure: a small, portly, dwarf-like creature, old and wrinkled, with a long white beard and a tatty green velvet jacket with a giant daffodil on his lapel over a chainmail breastplate. He was wearing yellow Bermuda shorts covered with palm trees that swayed in the thermal breeze.

'Hello!' said the dwarf in a helium-soaked squeal.

'Hello,' said Sparky.

'Lost?' squeaked the dwarf.

'Yes. Where am I?'

'This is the forest of the Coraniaid in the Valley of Grief. You should not be here! Who are you?'

'I'm Sparky. Who are you?'

'Pooface.'

'Excuse me?'

'My name is Pooface. Pooface Bumhole.'

'What? That's never your name.'

'It is.'

'You're lying.'

'I'm not.'

'You are.'

'Not so. Watch this!'

The dwarf screwed up his face and growled angrily, gritting his teeth and shaking his head and arms. His lips swung from cheek to cheek, saliva lobbing in all directions, his eyes rattling like pennies in a jam jar. The shaking got faster and faster until his head started spinning full circle, three hundred and sixty degrees. It whizzed so fast that all Sparky could make out was the fuzzy head of a violently spinning black toilet brush on the shoulders of the dwarf.

As it slowed, it began to take shape.

At first, Sparky thought it was a giant fruit, an apple. Then it faded to an orangey pink, like a peach. Its curves grew and inflated as he stared, then separated, until he realised he was glaring at a huge pair of hairy pink naked buttocks on the shoulders of the dwarf, its dirty brown anus in full view.

'See! See!' squealed the anus excitedly. 'Now. Your turn!'

'What do you mean?' asked Sparky, magnetised by the speaking bumhole.

'Show me you're real.'

'What? How?'

'I don't know. Let me see. Mmmm... Pull your foreskin over your head,' the anus squeaked.

'What?'

'You heard me. Pull your foreskin over your head. Then blow your nose.'

'I can't do that!' bawled Sparky. The pain intensified in his head.

The anus began to wink aggressively at him as the dwarf's body hopped foot to foot, jigging side to side. The anus started singing the chorus of Russ Abbott's 'Atmosphere' over and over, its squeal grating higher and higher as Sparky saw an apparition of Abbott's face smiling and singing along inside the giant daffodil petals on the dwarf's lapel.

The singing stopped and the forest fell silent. The anus started to hiss out whispers, 'Ssssparky, Ssssparky, Ssssparky.'

'So, it was you!' cried Sparky. 'What have I done to you? Why are you so horrible to me?'

The dwarf began to jig again as the anus squealed, 'I love you! I love you! I looove you!' The jigging stopped again suddenly. The buttocks faded to dark red, to purple, and the anus boomed, 'I JUST DON'T FUCKING LIKE YOU.'

Sparky let out a cry. He closed his eyes and slapped his face with his left hand, his right hand pressed to his burning gut. He looked up; the dwarf had gone, but the forest had come to life – branches, roots and vines began sliding, moving, slithering all around him, towards him. He stumbled forward, looking for signs of a path. But there was nothing.

He started to cough. He felt hot. He was sure his veins were swelling. His head felt like a pressure cooker ready to explode. He coughed again and blood splatted onto the palm of his dirty hand. He fell to the floor and coiled in on himself, coughing against the acrid taste of his own blood. His neck and face raged with heat and he struggled to breathe.

Daylight was approaching. Sparky could make out a huge swirl of black birds high up in the sky, circling over him, swarming closer and closer, just above the treeline. He heard their call, then – bats, thousands of them, swirling above his head in the faint morning light. He gasped as they began to nosedive, heading for him at pace like a cannon of crude oil, suddenly only yards away; he opened his mouth in terror and the bats flew straight into it, down his throat. Scores, hundreds, they kept coming – he was choking, but they didn't stop. Finally, he thrust his chest into the air and threw his head back. The whites of his eyes glowed and blood seeped from the corner of his mouth.

Chapter 11

At 10.49am, Biscuits and Boutros discovered Sparky's body, the bag of blue pills still clasped in his bruised left hand. Boutros pulled Biscuits in close and held him as he started to shake.

Within minutes, the search parties had been called over and everyone came crunching through the woodland to gather around Sparky in silence. His curly gold locks still looked so alive, and his bright red surf T-shirt illustrated with the words 'Live fast, die young, leave a nice-looking corpse in a nice pair of shorts' was clearly visible. John the Ghost knelt down and closed the boy's eyes.

Within an hour, the police and ambulance had arrived. Not far behind came rolling clouds. A new weather front was drifting in from the Atlantic like a grey blanket being slowly pulled over Pembrokeshire, dimming the morning minute by minute.

As the paramedics approached Sparky's body, Boutros realised that the bag of blue tablets had vanished from his hand. He frowned and looked around quickly, looking for a culprit but finding no one. As the police approached the scene, Boutros was torn, but he didn't mention the tablets during the questioning. This was an incident he didn't want to be drawn into, but his own silence kept him awake that night.

Sludge wouldn't come forward. He'd already been in enough trouble. And he was terrified of Ronnie. He had notified Biscuits to keep an eye on Sparky shortly after Ronnie had tossed him the pills. Sludge was worried – just that quarter of a pill had made him ill, overheat, vomit blood.. He knew Biscuits from Neyland Youth Club, back in the days, and he'd seen the pair of them leave the back of Gurnard's van just hours earlier, like cosmic cowboys, the universe their glittering oyster.

Biscuits didn't act. He didn't heed Sludge's warning. He'd been away on other planets himself. Sludge's words had drifted in and out of his mind that night, but in the morning they were definite and unshakeable. After the police questioning, Biscuits disappeared.

Toxicology results came back a week later, confirming that Sparky had taken a lethal dose of PMA, a toxic drug that had recently re-emerged as a cheap replacement for MDMA, the base ingredient of ecstasy. His death was attributed to an intracerebral haemorrhage that went on to cause hyperpyrexia, or overheating.

Without mention of the blue pills, nothing could be done. The police questioned and searched a number of known local drug dealers, but nothing was found and no one said a word. Ronnie's name was mentioned, but he had vanished.

Mostyn fully cooperated with the authorities and received a formal caution from the council for promoting an illegal commercial rave event. He escaped a hefty fine, apparently with the help of Mowbray.

Lewistock generated just over two thousand three hundred pounds. A failure, in light of the seven hundred-plus revellers that turned up on the night.

Weird Head paid Mostyn a visit on the farm the day after the rave to remind him he had just two days until payday, warned him that if the funds were not forthcoming he would crush his bones to dust.

Jethro had also disappeared, searching all over the county for Biscuits, but returned home from his failed mission on the night before the funeral.

The Price residence was one of Haverfordwest's finest. A Georgian manor set in large, impeccably groomed grounds with a grand entrance and a pristine tarmac drive. The property was surrounded by large oak and chestnut trees that dampened the outside noise, lending it a sense of rural living, yet it was only twelve minutes' walk to the high street and to the bank.

There was nobody home, so Daisy went around the side of the house, took the garage key from under the pebble and entered through the side door. She had to move quickly to catch the bus to St David's for the funeral.

She looked around the cluttered garage. The board had been moved into a corner and Ken the gardener had stacked his wheelbarrow, rake and shovel tightly between the board and Mr Price's black Jaguar E-Type.

'Fuckin' typical,' she moaned quietly, putting her hands on her hips. She took a deep breath and delicately lifted out the rake, then the shovel.

As she leaned over and clasped the hands of the wheelbarrow, she heard a car approaching the house.

'Bollocks,' she whispered. She didn't want to see Mr or Mrs Price. She hated them, weird stuck-up fuckers, never had anything to say to them, no common ground. Especially now, as she was about to dump their darling son, Dylan wonder boy Price. She glanced out of the garage window. It was Mr Price.

'Fuck it.' She pulled back the wheelbarrow, picked out the surfboard and leaned it against the dresser.

A second car, a burgundy Mitsubishi 4x4, drove in soon after. Daisy looked at the driver. Her heart sank.

'What the fuck?' She couldn't believe her eyes. Her mouth dried and she struggled to swallow. She looked around for somewhere to hide. There was nowhere. She delicately hopped over the wheelbarrow as the voices began to move towards the garage. She lay under the car, flat on the concrete, next to the wall, just as the metallic door handle squealed. The door was hoisted up and the two men entered. Daisy sensed an opportunity to jump up and play the fool, grab her board and skip off, but she missed it. She lay there stone-cold silent as Mr Price and Weird Head continued to speak.

'I've given you forty grand already since early June. When am I likely to see that back and more, for Christ's sake, Bev? I can't just keep dishing out cash to you willy fucking nilly.'

'Only joking, boss. Here. Here's six and a half grand. Got that all in one night at that rave last weekend. We should do more of 'em. The rest I'll be collecting this week. Probably in assets. I'll take them straight up to the shed at the farm, yeah?'

'Of course. Good.'

'I tell you, boss, it's not easy. These fuckers just aren't making their deadlines. I'm gonna have to properly turn the fuckin' screws in the next few days.'

'What do you mean?'

'Well, force the little bastards to pay us back.'

'And how do you plan on doing that? Don't you be going around hurting people and getting the hospitals and the pigs sniffing around again for fuck's sake. You're off your head if you go down that road. A kid has just fucking died. It's a small place down here, you know that. Don't think people aren't talking. They are. So keep your head down. And don't go thinking you're Mr Fucking Invincible either, because you're not.'

Daisy lay frozen. She tried to relax by breathing quietly and deeply, her mouth slightly open, piecing together the puzzle.

'Alright, alright, keep your fucking knickers on, boss. I get it.'

Daisy heard some movement and a key grate into a lock, the noise of the driver's door-lock popping open like the pull of a grenade pin.

Seconds later, the door slammed shut and the lock flipped back into place. The men continued talking as they walked out of the garage and closed it up. She heard the 4x4 leaving, but not the other car.

Daisy didn't move. She'd heard too much. Price was a freemason, a man of the community, in the *Western Telegraph* every second week dishing out giant cheques from the bank with his cheesy grin and slimy hair to scores of charities, schools and hospitals. He was odd, but that alone didn't make him the man who incited so much fear in his victims that they gave up their land, their livelihoods, even took their own lives.

Daisy thought of Colwyn, his ascent up the straw staircase to his gallows, the same bales he'd sown the seeds for, dressed, nurtured, harvested, removed from the field with his own hands.

She heard footsteps scurrying towards the garage. The door hoisted open again and the steps continued to the car. The driver's door opened and she felt the car pitch as Mr Price stepped in. The engine fired and roared. Daisy couldn't move. She lay there as the car rolled back out of the garage, revving aggressively.

The engine stabilised. Mr Price was staring coldly down at her on the floor. She felt the blood drain from her face. The engine stopped and Mr Price maintained his hollow stare in the silence. He opened the door. Daisy jumped up and skimmed across the wall, stopping at a white dresser strewn with sports kits and equipment. Price walked calmly and directly towards her, pulling the garage door down behind him as he entered.

'Hello, Daisy,' he said.

She didn't reply.

'What are you doing here, young lady?'

She felt her blood curdling. 'Nothing. I just came to pick up my surfboard.'

'I see. And how long have you been in here?'

'I just arrived this minute.'

'Hmmm. Why do I not believe you?'

She turned and ran for the side door. Mr Price followed and tackled her, knocking her to the ground, forcing his small greasy hand around her mouth.

'Get off me, you fucking psycho! Get off!' she screamed, wriggling from his grip. She stood up and stumbled towards the door. He pulled her back and punched her square in the face, knocking her off her feet. She fell back into the dresser. Blood seeped from her nose and she gasped for air.

'Now you listen to me, girl. You just tell me what you just heard and we'll talk about it and find a solution, alright? But believe you me, if you want to play fucking games with me, you will fucking regret it. Do you understand me?'

Daisy stared back at Mr Price. It was him. It had to be. The Growler. The evil bastard who'd stolen the money back from Colwyn and Mostyn. He knew them both well, their turmoil; he knew them as men and did nothing but seek to destroy them when they were most vulnerable, two of life's good men, for the sake of more money. She ground her teeth together. She had only met Rhys a few days ago, his young face showing the loss of his father. He was just a boy.

She grabbed a golf iron from a dusty golf bag next to the dresser and stepped quickly towards Mr Price, his eyes startled as the club thudded violently into his ribcage. The force threw him forward and his spectacles went flying. He hit the floor with a piercing shriek. He scrambled around for his glasses with his left hand as his right hand shielded his ribs.

'You fucking evil bastard!' screamed Daisy, her eyes sparkling, possessed with a will to damage as she widened her legs, raised both hands above her head and brought the golf club down with all of her force onto Mr Price's back. The loud thud went through her. She stepped back. He collapsed onto his stomach, wheezing, sucking wildly for air.

Daisy stood over him, , waiting for movement. He began to moan. Daisy kicked him in the face, full force. Blood oozed from his nose. Daisy stepped quickly over him and took her surfboard. As she reached the door, Mr Price jolted up onto his knees. 'I'm going to fucking kill you, bitch,' he hissed.

Daisy threw the board at him and ran. She was yards from the gates – she could hear his panting, his footsteps upon her, and she tried to run faster.

He tackled her and drove her at full force into the concrete gatepost. Daisy's head impacted first. Her legs crumpled as she lost consciousness.

Daisy couldn't say how long had passed when she came to in the boot of a car, as tight as a coffin, blindfolded, hands bound, her mouth gagged.

The boys often spoke about how they would like to be sent into the afterlife. Sparky had always fantasised about a surfer's burial, usually in the early hours after a big night out, as the chemicals faded and the bong worked its way around the sitting room. His fantasy never wavered. He'd seen videos of the ancient Polynesian custom in Hawaii, where local surfers paddled out at sunset to spread the ashes of fallen friends, warriors of the ocean. A big circle of watermen and women, holding hands as the spirit of the dead is released into the cradle of nature, back on its journey to the gods. Sparky wanted the same, just with his favourite tune, 'I am the Resurrection', thumping and grooving from giant speakers on the beach wall as his soul sailed away.

By 8pm, the crowds of mourners had all descended onto the beach, led by Rita, Sparky's mother. The sun dropped off the back of the ocean minutes later and the orange hour began. The horizon spread like a swirl of broken eggs to the south and north as big clouds formed around the bay, a guard of honour enriching the colours of the sky.

As Jethro pressed play on the sound system, the twenty-three surfers stepped onto the sand at Whitesands. The thumping singular drum of the song's opening whipped the surfers into a march towards the shoreline.

Mostyn was drawn to a group of four mourners standing on the headland on the south side of the lifeguard hut, right above the beach, all dressed in black. They looked ominous, like the four horsemen of the apocalypse, as the light began to fade around their gloomy silhouettes.

He squinted and saw they were all men. Then he noticed Weird Head. Mostyn had missed payday and now his heart began to race. He tried to attract Jethro's attention. Their eyes met. Mostyn gestured discreetly to the headland. Jethro looked up at the four men, then stepped quietly over to where Mostyn was standing, just five yards across the beach inside the crowd of young mourners.

'What are we going to do?' whispered Jethro from the side of his mouth, pitching his head towards Mostyn.

'I don't know. The deadline was a few days ago. They mean business now.'

'Looks like it. We can't go back to Lewis Mill. They'll fucking batter us to death.'

'I know.'

'How much was due?'

'Eight thousand. I've got two and a half. And forget trying to negotiate with him now.'

'You can't get any more, at all?'

'No.'

'Fuck.'

Both looked up at the headland and Weird Head waved down at them, flashing his sinister grin. They turned back and looked out to sea.

As the surfers waded into the ocean and dropped their boards onto the water, they separated, half going left, half right. They began to paddle around and formed a giant circle.

From the beach, Boutros was moved to tears by the aura of the ceremony. The sadness of all the young people reminded him of his own son, Matthew. He'd not seen him in twelve years, or even spoken to him once during that time, but every face on that beach was Matthew's.

Boutros had been absent to the point of irrelevance, extraneous as a father throughout Matthew's childhood and adolescent years as he was packed off, his sister Maggie also, to various boarding schools in Switzerland and England. Maggie flourished, qualified as a doctor and emigrated to New Zealand. But Matthew withered – he was lonely, isolated and bullied at every school. His father only found out years later. Boutros's failure to return home from mission to support his son in his battle against heroin addiction was the insufferable last act for Matthew, who shut his father out of his life on the day he left rehab.

Boutros was absorbed in a devastating cholera outbreak in rural Bangladesh at the time, far removed from his son's clinic in rural Buckinghamshire. He could have been granted compassionate leave from his duty station, but Dolly said Matthew was in good hands, and the cholera situation was severe, with staff resources already strained. Boutros chose not to leave. His rationale was that Matthew was in good care, under treatment, on the road to recovery. Matthew didn't see it that way. Same old story. Story of his father's life.

Matthew moved to Norway to be with a girl he'd met in school in Lausanne. They married, had two children, Freya and Peter, but Boutros had never set eyes on either of them. Matthew didn't even return for his own mother's funeral. Neither did Maggie. She was too busy, couldn't get away.

As the ropes had lowered Dolly's coffin deep into the soil, Boutros knew his life and what was left of it was now bereft of all meaning. He wished he'd had a gun, there and then, to end his misery, to fall into the earth and rest in peace with his Dolly for eternity.

Boutros wiped his eyes and looked back out to sea.

Right on cue, at three minutes and thirty-nine seconds into the record the surfers all sat up on their boards and joined hands as they rocked gently on the small swell. Jet-black silhouettes, a haze of amber illuminating them like a giant floating stone circle at dusk.

Jethro had never seen anything so moving, so intense, as the final jam of the record, a tour de force of harmony, groove and togetherness, seemed to rise up from the blazing sea itself.

His hairs stood on end as Deri paddled slowly into the middle of the circle, Sparky's ashes in an urn around his neck. He sat up on his board, took off the lid and raised the urn above his head. He screamed some words skywards that Jethro could not make out. The surfers all raised their joined hands and Deri threw Sparky's ashes up into the orange sky as the drums thumped and the guitars funked in their final throes. The entire beach stood breathless, mesmerised, as one of their own was returned.

Two minutes later, the music ended and the moment had passed, but the memory was stored forever in tiny treasure boxes in the minds of the young mourners that stood, still overwhelmed by the strange spirituality that lingered, engulfing the darkening peninsula.

The surfers began to paddle back to shore. The crowds remained scattered along the beach, gazing at the last glowing embers of the horizon, grieving, contemplating, reflecting.

As the crowds began to disperse from the beach, Jethro and Mostyn searched for an escape plan.

'I've got an idea,' said Jethro.

'I'm all ears, boy,' said Mostyn.

'There's a fucking treasure trove of tools and equipment up on this abandoned farm in the Preselis. Me and Biscuits stumbled upon it a few weeks ago.'

'And?'

'Well, we could easily lift five, six grand's worth of shit from there in an hour into the back of your horsebox, flog it and pay Weird Head.'

'What are you talking about? That stuff must belong to someone?'

'Probably. But seriously, this farm is abandoned, in the middle of nowhere, and I'm sure all that kit will never be used. There's shitloads. We can scope it out and if there's no one around, the loot is ours.'

Mostyn stood, thinking.

'What other options do we have, Most? We can shift it all quickly through some boys I know in Neyland, no worries.'

Jethro's breath caught in his throat. Weird Head and his mob were sauntering down the cliff path towards them. But Mostyn took off, walking straight in their direction.

'What the fuck are you doing?' shouted Jethro.

'Last orders tonight, Mariners, OK?' shouted Mostyn up to Weird Head as he raised his right hand and rubbed his thumb slowly in circles around the pads of his index and middle fingers.

Weird Head stared down at Mostyn for a moment and gave a slow singular nod through the scores of mourners making their way back to their cars.

Mostyn turned back to Jethro. 'Right, let's get a move on, boy. We gotta empty the horsebox.'

Part IV
Chapter 12

Daisy was woken by a loud thud above her.

Her nose and right cheek throbbed. Her hands were still tied, her mouth gagged, her blindfold in place, but she sensed the darkness, could almost smell it as she lay on the cold floor.

She put the left side of her face down and began to drag the blindfold against the wooden boards under her, trying to lift it. Thick dust wafted into her nose, making her sneeze. She caught the top of her cheek on a protruding nail and yelped. Blood swelled from the tiny wound. She used the nail to drag the blindfold as far as her forehead. Her left eye was released, but still she could see nothing.

She thought of her childhood, when she had preferred night to day. She would sit on the small cliffs at Druidstone, darkness soothing the sea as her father caught his last wave in the twilight. But at this moment, Daisy felt it filling her world, its open spaces, all its rooms and hidden drawers. She could not escape it.

Her eyes adjusted as she looked up out of the near-by window at the sky. Shadows passed across the half-moon. It was the blackest night of her life, yet the stars were bright. She ground her teeth on the gag and squeezed her eyes closed. She wouldn't let Mr Price decide her fate. She knew her father would be screaming at her, 'Fight, Dais. Look him in the eye and let him know you won't ever cede to the worthless bastard.'

Her heart slowed and she fell back to sleep.

Daisy awoke again at daybreak. She kept deadly silent for minutes, listening for sounds, the wind rolling under the doorways.

She looked around the dusty room, the house seemingly abandoned, trying to work out her location.

She sat up onto her knees and hooked her arm over the armrest of a brown fossilised sofa. She pulled herself up onto her feet and hopped across to the window. The menacing beauty of the view took her breath away. The Preseli Hills. She recognised the vast escarpment, like the curl of a giant wave.

She was near Pentre Ifan, the megalithic burial chamber where she and the boys would scurry around on their hands and knees, picking mushrooms as the October daylight faded after surfing the autumnal swells up north in Cardigan Bay. The mushrooms on this sacred ground carried the most psychedelic properties, according to local hippies, and the grass, as short as a putting green, made the clumps of small, nippled fungi easy to forage.

Daisy heard a car approaching the house. Her heart began to thump. She scooped out a chair from under the table with her right foot and sat on it, staring at the door.

Mr Price walked in with two white plastic shopping bags full of food and milk.

The loud thud that woke Daisy in the night now confused her. It couldn't have been him.

Mr Price was startled to see Daisy staring right at him, her nose bloodied, her face bruised, the gag cementing his return to his own nightmare.

Both were terrified by the other. Mr Price dragged out the chair opposite Daisy on the other side of the table and sat down.

'Are you alright?' he asked, a wobble in his voice.

Daisy nodded and attempted to speak, but the gag muffled her.

Mr Price walked cautiously around the table. 'It's OK, Daisy,' he said, untying the scarf and freeing her mouth. 'I won't hurt you.'

'My hands,' she said weakly, 'they really hurt.'

Mr Price looked down as she held them up submissively. They were purple on the tips.

'Oh, dear,' he said softly. He reached down and began to loosen the knot of the rope.

She sensed his nervousness. His hands trembled as he worked.

'What are you going to do to me?' she asked. He didn't look at her.

'I don't know. I really don't know. This is a nightmare. Bloody nightmare. It shouldn't have happened. What the hell were you doing in my garage? You shouldn't have been there!'

Mr Price knew he had crossed an invisible line, entered a place he thought he'd never go. He was so unprepared, but could see no way of retreating back into the life he'd left behind this. His eyes betrayed him.

Daisy knew a cornered beast was the most dangerous. 'I just came to collect my surfboard,' she said.

'Fucking surfboard? Jesus, shouldn't you be doing something useful? Fucking surfing,' he cursed.

Silence resumed as they sat like two lost souls in the dust of an abandoned saloon.

Mr Price heard the tiny pings of tinnitus electrify his ears for the first time in years. 'What exactly did you hear, Daisy?' he asked quietly.

Daisy stared at him, blinking, unsure of which path to take. 'I know you're the Growler,' she said finally.

'Pfff, the Growler. Fucking Growler!' he exclaimed as he slapped both his hands down hard on his lap. 'I didn't call myself that. So bloody stupid. Jesus.' He dragged his chair in tighter, still shaking his head. He leaned his head over the table towards Daisy, his nose twitching his glasses back up his nose. 'Look,' he said, almost in a whisper, 'all I do is just lend money to people who are unable to access finance from the banks. I know it's wrong, but it's not as if I'm bloody killing people.'

'What about Colwyn?'

'Look. Colwyn Morgan committed suicide. That's not my fault. He had it tough, but he could have worked his way back into solvency. His finances were not that bad.'

'You stole back the money you lent him.'

'What? What do you mean?'

'And from Mostyn.'

'What are you talking about, girl? Christ! It would be the end of my little enterprise if I fucked around like that, don't you think?'

Daisy paused, searching Mr Price's eyes. 'Well, that Weird Head must have done it then. Same thing. He works for you.'

'What the fuck are you talking about, Daisy?' His frown baffled her.

'You lent Mostyn and Colwyn twenty grand each, yeah?'

'Yes.'

'Well, within a day or two, both their houses were broken into and the money you lent them was all stolen back.'

His eyes darted from Daisy to the surface of the table, time and again. He rolled his fingertips on its top, waiting for a penny to drop.

Daisy could see he was not the thief.

'All forty grand?'

'Yes,' said Daisy.

'Jesus wept. That was nothing to do with me. I can assure you,' he said, slumping back in the chair and folding his arms. 'That fucker,' he whispered. 'I'll be honest with you, Daisy. I've been operating this black market of loans for about eighteen years now, and it's gone quite smoothly until recently. Yes, I've had to call in some of them and repossess a good few assets, but that has always been the deal if agreed obligations aren't met. Most of the time it's a win-win situation, and result.'

Daisy was only nineteen, but she believed there was darkness inside everyone, like yin and yang. Darkness in some more dangerously than in others, but she knew Mr Price was with the others.

'I'm sorry,' she said.

'What for?'

'Thinking you did all those things. I know you're not really capable of all that. Weird Head is giving you a bad name.'

'I'll deal with him.'

The tension slowly eased as Mr Price delved into one of the carrier bags, pulled out a banana and offered it to Daisy.

'You going to watch Dyl on Saturday? First game of the season,' Daisy asked, raising her hands to receive the fruit.

'Don't start with that now, Daisy. I'm not a fucking idiot.'

'What? It's a serious question.'

'Well, I'd love to, yes. But if I let you go and you go straight to the police, I'll be behind fucking bars before kick-off.'

'I won't. I give you my word,' she said firmly.

'Ha! With all due respect, Daisy, I know you're a good girl, but I can't risk my entire future on "your word". You're not even going with my son anymore. You're just a stranger to me now.'

'Shit, there's a car,' said Jethro.

Mostyn stopped the Land Rover. They were about two hundred yards from the house. Both of them remained silent, exhausted from a poor night of sleep in the horsebox. Mostyn spoke. 'It must just be in storage. Nobody will be staying there – look at the state of the place! And who the hell would drive an E-Type Jag all the way out to this bloody outpost before eight in the morning? There's not even any feeding up to do.'

'Yeah, you're probably right, but we'd better check it out first.'

They quietly reversed the Land Rover and horsebox back out onto the road and pulled in at the lay-by a little further down the hill towards the turning for Pentre Ifan.

They kept their feet light as they walked down the lane and out onto the moor that led to the farm, the stunning black sports car positioned ominously in the wasteland.

Mostyn's eyes were drawn to the starkness of the vast plain and the distant escarpment, both lit up by the broken sunshine, the path towards the farm lying in shadow.

They slunk around to the pine end before peeping through each window as they slowly circumnavigated the house.

'Get down!' Mostyn grabbed Jethro's arm.

'What? What?' Jethro whispered, their backs pushed against the wall.

'I don't know if I'm seeing things,' said Mostyn, trembling, 'but I think Daisy is in there, with Mr Price.'

'What?' He slid his eye slowly off the wall and the two came into view through the clouded pane, sitting at opposite ends of a table, eating. 'I think her hands are tied,' he whispered desperately. 'What the fuck is going on, Mostyn?'

Mostyn pulled him back and they scurried to the pine end of the house.

'He's fucking kidnapped her! I'm gonna snap his fucking neck.'

Jethro scanned the ground for an implement, a weapon.

'Steady on now, boy.' Mostyn grabbed Jethro again firmly. Jethro was startled by Mostyn's strength and could see the fear in the old man's eyes. His bravado gave way as they tucked back in tight against the wall.

'I don't get it, Most? Why the fuck are they here? Here!'

'I don't know, boy. You sure she's tied up? Maybe they're having a fling?'

'What the fuck are you talking about?' Jethro turned on Mostyn. 'That's my girlfriend in there. She's a fucking hostage! We've got to go in there. Now.'

They stared at each other for a moment. 'You're right. Sorry, boy. But we need a plan. We don't know the situation. Maybe there are more people in there.'

'What kind of plan?'

'I don't know. Tell Price we know what's going on, we followed them here, and the place is surrounded with coppers.'

'Fine. Whatever. It's just the two of them in there. Has to be,' he said, pointing at the car. 'I just say we kill the bastard if he's laid a finger on Daisy.'

'Hey, stop that talk,' said Mostyn. 'You may as well dig two graves if you go down that road. One for him and one for yourself, even if you get out alive.'

'Alright, alright,' said Jethro. 'Come on.'

They tiptoed to the furthest door from the room where Daisy and Mr Price were sitting. Jethro picked up a length of rusted steel piping that was lying on the broken concrete path. Mostyn didn't say a word. The half-rotten door was ajar, caught in overgrowth. Jethro began to rock the door backwards and forwards, loosening it from the clutches of earth and grass.

When they stepped into the house, Jethro stopped dead. He'd woken in this exact room only a few weeks ago. Life was bad then, but it was a lot worse now. He felt his airways contracting. His hands went clammy. He hesitated to step forward.

Mostyn cast him a fatherly look, raised his eyebrows and silently mouthed, 'OK?' Jethro nodded solemnly.

They moved quietly through the room and entered the hallway, the trunk of the house from which all rooms branched. They could hear the muffled voices of Daisy and Mr Price getting louder as they shuffled down the corridor towards them.

They reached the doorway. Jethro slowly stretched his head around the half-closed door and the back of Mr Price came into view. Daisy was facing Mr Price, looking in Jethro's direction. She was eating a biscuit. He didn't want to startle her, but he took in the damage. He was ready to kill. Jethro exposed more of his head and Daisy's eyes finally moved upwards. Their eyes met. She shot a glance back at Mr Price. Her sudden movement jolted him and she could see he sensed danger. Daisy could not help but glance back up at Jethro. Mr Price spun around in his chair, but he was not quick enough to block the blow of the rusted pipe. He screamed out and fell to the floor, clutching his throat. Jethro ran to Daisy and began to untie her hands.

Mostyn stood over Mr Price, holding a big glass bottle by its neck, half raised, ready to act.

Jethro was frantic. 'What happened, Dais? What the fuck's going on?' He tried to focus, one eye on the knot, one eye on Mr Price, writhing on the floor.

'He's the Growler. He's the Growler!' Daisy cried out as Jethro freed her hands. She stood up and fell into his arms.

'What do you mean, Daisy?' asked Mostyn.

'I overheard him and Weird Head. I was in his garage getting my surfboard yesterday and they came in. I hid, but he saw me. He put me in the boot.'

She broke down.

Jethro held her tightly and stroked her sodden face, trying to calm her.

Mostyn's face darkened. He couldn't believe it. That was impossible. The Growler was supposed to be huge, the king of the underworld, the lord and master of Weird Head. How could this be? This little slimy man. In his heels. His twitches. His nerves. Price knew them so well, him and Col. How could a man possibly do that to another?

'Is this true, Price?' Is it fucking true?'

Mr Price nodded, clutching his smashed Adam's apple, his body convulsing as he tried to swallow.

The image of Colwyn swinging by his neck hurtled into Mostyn's mind. He wanted to stamp on Price's head, to stamp it to pieces. But then he saw his father and mother, sat alone at the pew with dignity after Gareth's passing. He pulled himself back, took a deep breath.

'But I didn't take it back,' said Mr Price between wheezes. 'I promise you, Mostyn. It wasn't me.'

Mostyn glared back at Daisy. 'What's he talking about?'

'He says he didn't steal back the money. I believe him. It must have been Weird Head by himself,' she said.

Mostyn put the bottle down on the table and rubbed his face with his hands. He didn't know how much more he could take.

'Fuck, there's a jeep coming up the lane!' yelled Jethro.

Daisy shot a glance out of the window. It was the burgundy Mitsubishi 4x4, this time pulling a horsebox. Weird Head was behind the wheel.

'Fuck, speak of the devil.'

Jethro scanned the room. 'Quick, tie that fucker up.' He threw Daisy's gag at Mostyn. Mostyn bent down cautiously. He could see Mr Price was struggling.

'I'm just going to tie you up as a precaution. I'll try not to put you in any more pain,' said Mostyn. He'd calmed. Price was vile, but Weird Head was evil. And he was, for reasons unknown to Mostyn, pulling up right outside at this very moment.

'Right, upstairs!' exclaimed Jethro. He moved to Mr Price and slid his arms under his armpits, hoisted him up and dragged him out through the door towards the staircase. The rasp of Mr Price's cough echoed up to the landing as blood filled the joins of his teeth. Daisy followed closely.

They dragged Mr Price into a back bedroom. Mostyn and Jethro shot back to the landing to follow Weird Head's movement. He'd pulled up and was flicking open the bolts at the back of his horsebox. He dropped the gate and walked calmly in through the front door of the house.

'If you make a sound, I'll rip your fucking throat out,' hissed Jethro into Mr Price's ear.

Mr Price nodded. He was barely conscious.

'Boss, you here?' Weird Head shouted. 'Boss?' He fingered around inside the bags of food and took a pack of biscuits, then returned to the horsebox and began unloading.

'That's my fucking lawnmower, I'm sure of it,' whispered Mostyn. Weird Head was dragging it over towards the shed. Then he pulled out two of Mostyn's toolboxes, Mostyn's drill sets, Mostyn's vice. 'Bastard.'

Judging by the strained noises, there must have been something heavy at the front end of the horsebox. Even inside the house they could hear Weird Head's curses and bursts of breath, loud thuds rattling the frame of the horsebox.

Mostyn and Jethro watched through the clouded upstairs window, waiting for Weird Head to finish his work and leave.

'You want a hand there, Bev?' A new voice rippled through the yard.

Mostyn's and Jethro's eyes swept across to the small outbuilding. Ronnie was standing in the doorway.

Chapter 13

'What the fuck are you doing here?' asked Weird Head.

'What do you mean? Just lying low.'

'The pigs are on to you, you know? You need to make yourself scarce. For a fucking long time.'

'Why?'

'Those blue pills, you twat. Sludge has been talking. I dunno if it's got back to the pigs yet, but it will. What the fuck did you give them to that kid for?'

'It wasn't me. I didn't fucking do it. It was Sludge, that little fat fuck,' said Ronnie. His expression unnerved Weird Head.

'Look, whatever. It's not my problem. Do what the fuck you like. Just give us a hand here to pull this fucking engine out, will you? It's like a lump of fucking lead.'

Ronnie sauntered across the yard and climbed into the back of the horsebox. Within a minute, they had dragged the engine out to the top of the ramp, in full view. It was Mostyn's vintage stationary engine, the Lister D, bought for him by his father. They had restored it together during the five years of the war, as a distraction from the turmoil of the world beyond theirs. The sight of the two criminals rough-handling his last meaningful link to his father was unbearable. Mostyn shuffled backwards quickly in retreat, but his heels hit the rise of the doorway and he fell backwards, collapsing on the hard wooden floorboards.

Weird Head and Ronnie looked up.

'That you, boss?' shouted Weird Head.

No reply.

'Boss, come and check out this fucking engine. It's older than you.'

No reply.

Weird Head frowned at Ronnie. 'That's weird. You must have seen him or heard him, no?'

'Nope. I've made myself a little den at the back of that little shed there, insulated with straw bales. I've not heard fuck all for days.'

Weird Head clanged down the ramp and marched into the house.

Mostyn and Jethro shuffled back into the bedroom where Mr Price lay. Jethro held Daisy tight, the steel pipe clasped so tightly in his right hand that his knuckles whitened.

'Big bad Mr Growler? You up there?'

No response.

Weird Head thudded lazily up the stairs.

Mr Price moved, banging his knee on the floor. Weird Head glanced up at the door. He grabbed a pewter candlestick from the dresser on the landing, reached the door and pushed it open with his boot.

'Well, fuck me sideways,' he said.

Mostyn, Jethro and Daisy stood frozen. Jethro had the pipe at full tilt, ready to swing.

'Ron, Ron, get up here, quick,' Weird Head shouted, 'we've got company.'

Jethro willed himself to swing, but couldn't. Weird Head was massive, his neck as thick as a seal's. If he failed to knock him out, they would all be dead, Jethro was sure.

Ronnie appeared in the doorway next to Weird Head. 'Well, well, well. What the fuck have we here then? Am I seeing things, Bev?'

'No, Ronald, I believe you are not,' said Weird Head, staring coldly into Mostyn's eyes. 'Drop it,' he said to Jethro. Jethro let the pipe fall, clattering against the boards.

'Amazing,' said Ronnie. 'The hunted throwing themselves into the mouths of the hunters. So where's the catch, you fucking idiots?'

Seconds of silence passed like days.

'The police are outside. They sent us in,' said Mostyn.

Weird Head and Ronnie considered the claim. 'Why would they send all three of you muppets in here?' asked Weird Head. 'And who's this little hussy? Does she need to be here, risking her life? I don't think so.' He grinned.

Weird Head heard wheezing and stepped cautiously into the room. He looked around the side of the bed and saw Mr Price, hearing the sound of his collapsed throat as he desperately tried to breathe.

'Jesus Christ.' He turned to Jethro. 'Did you do that to him?'

Jethro nodded.

'Fair play, that's a hell of a fucking strike there, boy.' Weird Head crouched down close to Mr Price. 'You alright down there, boss?' He patted him on the back. Ronnie sniggered.

Mostyn was stunned. He saw they were both sick in the heart.

'Help me, Bev. Please. Get me to Withybush,' Mr Price said between gasps.

'It's not as simple as that, boss. You see, these two clowns owe me and Ron here lots and lots of cash, and we need to sort that out as a priority. They've been fucking us around for weeks now, eh, Ron?'

'They certainly have, Mr Weird Head. Young Tarzan over there owes me two grand. Missed his first deadline. Silly boy.'

'You can't be having that, Ron,' mocked Weird Head, enjoying himself.

'I can't,' he replied. Ronnie revealed a Colt .45 from his waistband, lifting the barrel of the handgun towards them.

'Don't be flaunting that about, Ron,' Weird Head said. 'If that thing goes off, we'll have company pretty fucking quick.'

'Will we fuck,' Ronnie said. 'There's nothing around for miles. I could spray these cunts with a Gatling gun out there on the moors and no one would ever know.'

'Let's just simmer down here now, kids,' said Weird Head, patting his right hand towards the gun. 'Let's take some time to review this very unique situation.' He waved his candlestick, gesturing the three hostages to move downstairs. Ronnie stood back, his gun now hanging down by his side, his finger still on the trigger.

Weird Head tied their hands tightly behind their backs and sat the three of them down on the old settee in the kitchen. Weird Head and Ronnie pulled up two kitchen chairs and sat less than two metres away across the hearth of the ancient chimney breast.

'So?' said Weird Head.

There was only silence.

'Answer me, you pair of pricks, otherwise you'll both be joining that stupid old twat Trevor in hell.'

Jethro's face hardened.

'What do you want to know?' asked Mostyn.

'What the fuck are you doing here for a start? I'm intrigued,' said Weird Head.

'We came to take some of the tools from that shed. To sell. To pay you back,' said Jethro calmly.

'Well, you dirty little tea leaf. Ironically, those tools in that shed belong to me and the gaffer, rolling around on the floor up there. And anyway, how the fuck do you know about this place?'

'We came across it after a party up in the commune behind Newport. We were on foot, got lost and needed to find shelter, somewhere to sleep.'

'Fuck me, you sound like the wild man of the fucking Amazon, boy. And you, Mostyn. What are we going to do with you, old boy?' said Weird Head, folding his arms in warm anticipation.

'I'm selling the farm. You'll have your money as soon as I do, with interest.'

'Oooh. Now you're talking.'

'Just please don't damage that engine,' said Mostyn, his voice wavering.

'Why's that, old boy? Precious, is it?'

'My father gave it to me. We restored it together.'

'Aww, bless. Hear that, Ron? Mostyn and Daddy restored that fucking old hunk of shit on the box out there.'

Ronnie smirked and left the room. His footsteps crunched across the yard and then banged up the ramp of the horsebox. There was a crash as the engine tumbled down the ramp, smashing onto the concrete yard below. Mostyn dropped his head.

'You'll have to excuse my friend Ron, there. He's a bit of a psychopath, you see.' Weird Head began to chuckle.

Mostyn looked up again, straight at him. 'You sick bastards.'

Jethro closed his eyes.

'Excuse me, Worzel Gummidge?'

'You heard me. You're not human.'

Weird Head's face hardened. 'Watch your mouth, farmer boy.'

'I'm not afraid of you, you piece of shit.'

Weird Head dragged his chair six inches closer towards Mostyn and punched him square on the nose.

Daisy yelped, closing her eyes tightly.

The force threw Mostyn back into the cushion. Blood seeped from both nostrils, but he didn't make a sound. He slowly sat up and stared coldly at Weird Head. Weird Head nodded and huffed. 'So pissypants finally grew some balls. Huh. I have to say I'm quite proud of you, Mostyn.' Their eyes locked until Weird Head broke off and strode out of the room.

Minutes later, he returned with a length of rope and tied Mostyn's, Jethro's and Daisy's legs together.

'Sit tight now, my three musketeers,' he said, patting Mostyn firmly on the cheek. 'Any funny business and I'll let Ron have his way with you. You understand?'

Jethro and Daisy nodded.

'What about Price?' asked Mostyn firmly. There had not been a sound from him for over half an hour.

'Fuck that little weasel,' said Weird Head, strolling into the hallway and closing the door behind him. He went outside, walked across to the storage shed and slid open the big red wooden door. The shriek of the door sliding over the rusted rollers made Ronnie wince.

'Give us a hand here, Ron. Gotta move some of this shit around. Getting full in here now.'

Ronnie huffed and sauntered over.

Footsteps moved quickly upstairs.

Jethro frowned at Mostyn.

The steps continued. They ran down the stairs, skipped across the hallway and bolted straight out through the front door.

'Price?' quizzed Jethro.

'Can't be, he's half dead,' said Mostyn.

'I know, but it has to be. He must have been putting it on a bit or something. He's no fucking idiot,' said Jethro.

'I dunno,' said Mostyn. 'He was in a bad way.'

'I think there could have been someone else up there,' said Daisy flatly.

Jethro turned sharply and looked at her. 'What?'

'Last night I heard a thud upstairs. It woke me up. Price only came back this morning.'

'What, just one thud?'

'Yep. Nothing more.'

'Did you go back to sleep after you heard it?' asked Jethro.

'Yeah, for a couple of hours probably.'

'If it was anything, it must have been Price then. He probably left when you fell back to sleep.'

'Fuck, I dunno,' said Daisy with a big sigh. 'Maybe it was nothing.' She rested her head on Jethro's shoulder, and they all sat in silence.

'OK, just by here will do, John,' said Biscuits.

John the Ghost pulled the pick-up into the lay-by and Biscuits jumped out. He had a packed rucksack and a plastic bag full of sticks and splintered logs.

'So, thirty minutes max, yeah?' said Biscuits, leaning his head back through the open passenger-side window.

'Yep. Roger. Don't worry, it's all clear, by three o'clock I'll be long gone,' said John.

'Tidy,' said Biscuits.

'You sure you know what you're doing now, boy? Don't be putting the three of them at risk. You know we should just call the police.'

'Fuck that. Waste of time. The pigs won't find much on them. Then they'll just torture us all for the rest of our lives. They need a taste of their own medicine.'

John saw a changed boy, but felt pride at his courage. John knew well the evil of passivity, to never intervene.

'Be careful, son,' said John firmly.

Biscuits smirked. 'I'll be just fine, John the Ghost.'

The red pick-up bounced across the lane and out on to the moor towards the abandoned farm and Weird Head came breezing out of the shed. Ronnie slunk back into his den like a rat.

John pulled up, stepped out and walked across to meet Weird Head. 'Alright, Candyman.'

'What the fuck are you doing here? I don't need any pick-ups now for a while.'

'Sorry, man. I'm just desperately looking for some tools. Thought you could help me out.'

'That's John the fucking Ghost!' exclaimed Jethro.

'Sshhh!' said Mostyn, listening intently.

'Yeah, well, it's not a convenient time now, pal. I'm just doing my inventory. I'll copy you tomorrow once I'm all sorted.' Weird Head was agitated, shooting glances across to the house.

'Let's shout, fucking scream, do something!' said Jethro hysterically.

'No!' said Daisy. 'Ronnie's got a fucking gun out there. It's too dangerous.'

'Oh, come on, man, I've bloody driven up here from Nolton. Jim Bevan's baler's broken down and it's giving rain from tomorrow. Muggins here is the only one who can fix it, but my tools are up with my cousin in fucking Swansea. I've got cash.' He pulled out a fair wad. 'I'll pay you a good whack if you've got what I need.' He strummed his dirty thumb across the notes under Weird Head's nose.

Weird Head considered. 'Alright,' he said, and pushed John towards the shed, away from the house, 'but fucking hurry up. I've got shitloads to sort out here today.'

John took his time in the shed, picking out a variety of spanners, wrenches, socket sets and screwdrivers. Weird Head watched him closely. They agreed a price and the transaction was made. John kept talking, small talk, rubbish, until Weird Head ran out of patience. 'Right, can you just fuck off now please, Strummer Boy? I've got to crack on.'

It was enough time for Biscuits to finish his work out on the moor, out on the edge of the bog.

As the pick-up revved its engine and John drove out of the farmyard,

Biscuits retreated to the trees on the boundary of the moor and lay in the long grass, going methodically through his plan. Everything was in place. He waited.

At around 6pm, Biscuits opened a can of cider, took a long swig and carefully unfolded a wrap of speed with his trembling fingers. He lined the open crease of the wrap directly into the can and let out a 'Whee!' as the white powder tumbled into the fizzy cider.

Within five minutes, the can was empty. He was dehydrated, so drank another, then another, as the daylight faded and the amphetamines surged through him. He felt bold. He was going to save his friends, or go down in flames.

Weird Head and Ronnie came back into the house at around 8pm.

'Still here?' joked Weird Head.

Mostyn cleared his dry, dusty throat. 'Could we have some water, please?'

'Water. Ah yeah, let me see.' Weird Head looked around the old kitchen, the shadows growing. He took one of the dust-caked glass bottles off the kitchen table and went outside, sank the bottle in the half-full concrete water trough in the back yard and then returned to the kitchen. 'Here. This is all that's here, old boy.' He offered it to Mostyn with a smile.

'No thanks.'

'I thought you shitkickers always drank from cow troughs?'

Mostyn looked away and sighed.

'Can we have some of that milk, please?' asked Daisy softly.

'That was very polite, sugar tits. Of course you can.' He took out a bottle from Mr Price's carrier bag, opened the top and took it over to the settee. He gave them each a good glug of the milk. 'Look at me, like Mother fuckin' Teresa to you lot.'

'Price is still alive,' said Mostyn. 'He's been moving around. Maybe he should have some fluids as well.'

'Fuck me. I'm gonna put you forward for the Nobel Peace Prize, Mostyn. You actually care about that slimy little fuck?'

Mostyn didn't reply.

Weird Head went upstairs. Mumbles and groans vibrated through the floorboards into the kitchen. He returned less than a minute later. 'He'll survive. Sadly.' Weird Head began scratching his head.

'Right, Ron, I'm gonna nip home, feed the lodger, then pop to Tommy Harries for supplies. Back around ten. Keep an eye on these little fuckers, alright?'

'I think I can manage that,' Ronnie said, surveying the hostages.

As Weird Head turned for the door, it burst open. Biscuits came charging in.

'You fucking murdering cunts!' he screamed towards Jethro and Mostyn. They both felt the length of the two-by-four Biscuits was wielding. 'You killed Sparky. That fucking rave killed him!' The muscles in his jaw pulsated. 'I'm gonna kill you!' He let the length of wood drop and resorted to his hands. Blood ran from Jethro's nose and red bruises were soon forming on Mostyn's haggard face.

Weird Head and Ronnie stood frozen, frowning, bamboozled.

Biscuits turned to them. 'Who the fuck are you?' he screamed.

'Hold your fucking horses there now, boy,' said Weird Head, gesturing to Biscuits to calm down with his big hands. 'Who the fuck are you?'

'That's his mate. I've seen you two together before,' said Ronnie, linking Jethro to Biscuits with a limp, wagging finger.

'Was my best mate, until those two selfish greedy bastards decided to throw that rave. My friend died! It's all their fucking fault!' He kicked Mostyn and Jethro in the shins.

'Fucking calm down there, squire,' boomed Weird Head.

Biscuits pulled back, hyperventilating. He gritted his teeth and growled viciously at Jethro and Mostyn.

They both stared up at Biscuits. Daisy sobbed uncontrollably.

Biscuits regained his breath. He turned to Weird Head. 'What you planning on doing with these bastards?' he asked. 'Count me in. Whatever.'

Weird Head's mind set to work; he could offload the job onto this kid and walk away scot-free. 'Not sure yet, but that's good to know, kid. What's your name?'

'Biscuits.'

'Biscuits?' Weird Head laughed. He looked at Ronnie and they both began to chuckle.

'Don't laugh, you fuckheads, otherwise I'll do the pair of you too.'

Weird Head and Ronnie exploded with laughter at the ridiculous little teenager, five foot nothing with girl's hair, offering them out.

'I'm not fucking kidding,' continued Biscuits.

Weird Head clasped his stomach and went on laughing.

Biscuits swung off his heavy rucksack. 'Right, who wants a cider?' he demanded, unclipping his bag and pulling out six cans. He cracked one open and sucked it down in one, letting out an almighty 'Ahhhh!' as the bubbles rolled down his gullet.

'You're not right in the fuckin' head, boy,' said Weird Head. 'Yeah, chuck us one, I'm fucking gagging.'

'Me too,' said Ronnie.

Biscuits tossed them both a can, carried over the remaining three and placed them on the filthy stone sink. Biscuits fired question after nonsensical question, cracking jokes, keeping them amused. He was off his face. His concoction of speed, cider and surging adrenaline was a gregarious mix, disarming Weird Head and Ronnie. They couldn't get a word in edgeways.

Mr Price started banging loudly upstairs and calling out for help.

'Fuckin' hell,' moaned Weird Head, rolling his eyes. 'What's wrong with that old cunt now?' He headed upstairs.

Ronnie moved towards the carrier bags on the table and rummaged inside for some food. 'Alright up there, Bev?'

Weird Head started on a long monologue about soft-arse, slimy, bent bank managers. This was Biscuits' moment. He walked over to the sink and quickly opened three more cans of cider. He whipped out the small money bag from his T-shirt pocket and emptied the contents equally into two of the cans: twenty microdots. He started singing Happy Mondays' 'Hallelujah' as he swirled the cans around in his hands, dissolving the LSD.

'Candles. Tidy,' mumbled Ronnie, taking six from the bag and lighting two of them. He melted the base of each with the flame of the other and set them on the kitchen table in the middle of the room. The effect was instant, the glow radiating up onto Ronnie's lone figure as he stood in the decaying room.

Biscuits turned around as Weird Head stomped back down the stairs. He was there to welcome him with a fresh can of cider as he strode back into the kitchen. Ronnie snatched his can from Biscuits without a word.

Biscuits' singing got louder, more exaggerated, even intimidating, as he did his baggy Madchester dance over to the settee, arms up, fingers spread, his body rolling from side to side, then lunged his head aggressively at Jethro and winked.

Jethro jerked back, startled. His mind raced.

Biscuits continued to sing and dance around the kitchen while Weird Head and Ronnie sucked down their second cans quickly in silence, still amused by the spectacle.

Within twenty minutes, the drugs began to take effect. Within forty minutes, Weird Head and Ronnie were losing their minds.

Chapter 14

Biscuits was sitting quietly on the kitchen table, swinging his legs like a contented toddler, supping on another can of cider and dabbing speed.

There had been a tetchy thirty minutes as the tsunami of LSD surged into Weird Head's and Ronnie's brains, making them lash out sporadically, ferociously, as they edged their way into the corner of the old kitchen.

Biscuits went and sat on the arm of the settee, his head bowed, allowing them the space to descend into their own madness.

Jethro soon realised what was going on, but Biscuits ignored his whispers.

Weird Head and Ronnie let out gasps as they began to lose their hold on the world they inhabited. Within an hour and a half, all panic had gone and they were both clinging to the old Aga, whispering and jabbering to themselves.

Biscuits called over to them to sit down around the table and to breathe deeply. They obeyed, dragged out a chair each, sat down and placed their elbows on the table. Their eyes were remote, out there, air wheezing and rattling out of their lungs.

The small spherical glow of the candlelight encompassed Ronnie. He held both hands up in front of his nose and began slowly wiggling his fingers. He looked elated, his smile wide and honest.

'Are they really my hands?' he asked.

'Yes, Ronnie. They appear to be attached to your arms, so they must be,' said Biscuits.

Jethro and Daisy sniggered.

Mostyn looked confused.

Weird Head sat in silence for a long while. He was busy playing Tetris on the kitchen table with the luminous blocks that were raining slowly down from the sky. He looked up and his voice tore through the silence. 'Fucking hell, Ron, you've got tits!'

Ronnie pounced from his chair. 'What? What? What's the twits?' He was frantically brushing down his arms and sides, then his head, his backside and legs, trying to sweep the twits off him, whatever they were.

Biscuits buckled with laughter and stood up. 'The twits, the twits, Ronnie's got the twits!' He crept towards Ronnie. 'Twiiitsss, twiiitsss, twiiitsssssssss,' he hissed. He continued to whisper it, time and again, just loud enough for Ronnie to perceive as he tried to blink himself back to normality. He was en route to full meltdown.

Weird Head had sunk back in his chair, his hands on his knees, staring at the floor, mouthing words quietly to himself. He pulled his head up quickly, as if he'd just woken, and flashed a glance over his shoulder at the draining board. 'Is there a plate with fucking rabbits on the draining board over there?' he asked nervously.

Biscuits hopped off the table and swaggered over. 'Yes, there is, Mr Cleverclogs.' He held up the dust-covered children's dinner plate to Weird Head and grinned.

Weird Head let out a strange noise, a sound of fear. 'I just came out of my body. I was up on the ceiling. I looked over and saw that plate.' He tried shaking his head clear. The anxiety subsided quickly and he drifted off, as though on a wave of serene dementia, on to his next adventure.

John the Ghost had told Biscuits all about Weird Head and Ronnie on the drive up to the hills that afternoon. Two devout drug-free criminals who were more than happy to peddle lethal chemicals to teenagers for the right price.

Ronnie was a small-time crook who came from a small town in Scotland, John forgot which one, around ten years ago, fleeing big debts he could not honour to bad people. That probably explained why he lived in a caravan at the end of a lonely lane on old Ernest George's farm, Treffiddin, out near St Justinian's, the end of the road.

When he arrived, Ronnie was paranoid. He'd lost all of his hair to alopecia. People had come after him, small gangs of intimidating Scots, asking questions around the pubs of Haverfordwest and St David's, some calling for 'Paedo-Ron'. Word had it that he had spent time in prison for molesting children in his own family, and that he was still very much a wanted man, outside of the law. His isolation in the caravan made sense. There, he was invisible.

But within a couple of years, Ronnie had become more comfortable, slowly calculating his own re-emergence. He'd met Weird Head in strange circumstances, both of them poaching for salmon in the depths of the night near Black Tar, a section of the Cleddau known for bountiful catches in the autumn months. After a short stand-off, they both sensed a potential use for the other in developing their unconventional activities.

Weird Head and the Growler, whose identity John didn't know until Biscuits informed him on the drive up, had been working together for well over a decade. What seemingly began as a semi-well-intentioned yet high-interest micro-credit cash-based enterprise turned more sinister within a year of Ronnie entering the fray. Profits were diverted to finance a growing illegal trading realm of drugs, farm machinery and small firearms.

The Growler was apparently kept in the dark about this diversification of activities, and by the time he was fully aware, it was too late for him to walk away. He was a local dignitary, an upstanding man of the community, and Weird Head had him by the short and curlies.

'What have you spiked them with, Biscuits?' Jethro asked again.

'Microdots, boyo.'

'How many?'

'Twenty between them, but one of them may have had slightly more than the other.' He grinned.

'Jesus. Well, you can fucking untie us now then, Sergeant fucking Pepper.' Jethro was livid. 'Why the fuck did you batter us like that, you fucking tool?'

'I had to.'

'You didn't have to nearly break our fucking bones, for fuck's sake.'

'J, if I'd have done it half-arsed, they'd have sniffed it and we'd all be lined up on death row down there.'

'He's right,' said Mostyn. 'Fair play, boy, you had me there. You've made me feel like a murderer now though.'

'No, no, sorry, Mostyn, that was just a pile of horseshit. I didn't mean that. It was the only thing I could think of,' said Biscuits.

Mostyn nodded a sad smile and looked down.

'Cut these ropes then, Biscuits,' said Jethro, his patience waning.

'Nope.'

'What?'

'You're staying put.'

'Don't fuck about now, you dick, just because you're off your tits. Just cut these ropes. Our wrists are fucking bleeding here.'

Biscuits walked up to the sofa and looked straight at Jethro. 'J, I've got a job to do, a few scores to settle. For us all.' Biscuits became agitated. 'I heard those cunts this morning. I was upstairs. Been holed up here for days now. Heard the fucking lot. Pushing Mostyn's engine out of that horsebox was the last straw. Those bastards are going to die tonight.' The thick veins in his neck were bulging as he glared across the candlelight at the two mobsters.

'What do you mean?' asked Jethro.

'It means I'm gonna fuckin' kill them, Jethro.'

'Don't be a fucking twat, Biscuits. Don't talk like that.'

'What am I supposed to do, J? For fuck's sake. Look at this fucked situation. We're fucked either way. I'm gonna do them.'

'You sound like your father,' said Jethro softly.

'Yeah, yeah. Nice. Go fuck yourself, Jethro.' Biscuits' body deflated as he stood before the three of them. 'What the fuck did I do? WHAT THE FUCK DID I DO?' He screamed so loud that Ronnie and Weird Head looked up, before their heads slowly meandered back down. 'You know me! I was full of peace and love. More than anyone. But now I just fantasise of damage, violence and fucking revenge. And the funny thing is, none of it's my fault! I didn't ask for my old man to torment me, or break my fucking nose. I didn't ask for Sparky to die. I didn't give him those dodgy pills.' Biscuits stopped and dropped his head, grinding down on the inside of his cheeks powerfully enough to draw blood.

'We know, Biscuits,' said Mostyn. 'We know you're a good kid. You've got nothing to be ashamed of, but killing those two men is not going to make everything right now, is it?'

'Yes, it will. They deserve it. I don't know why you're all against me. They killed your friend Colwyn and Sparky. They're fucking murderers!'

'Maybe so, but that doesn't give you the right to decide to end their lives for them, does it? "Though shalt not kill" it says in the scriptures.'

'Fuck the scriptures. I don't believe in anything,' he snapped. 'You bloody Christians, it's all about reward or punishment, isn't it?'

'What do you mean?' asked Mostyn.

'The lot of you, you'd only not kill because you're scared to go to hell, not because you're nice. That's right, isn't it?'

'What are you talking about, boy?' Mostyn had never before heard anyone question the integrity of his faith.

'Stop it, Biscuits,' said Daisy.

'Even if you don't have faith, Biscuits,' Mostyn said, 'there's a set of morals that we should all adhere to, as human beings.'

'Yeah, well, maybe those morals don't make sense to everyone in the same way.'

'What do you mean?'

'Well, I'm sure an old farmer from yesteryear has a different set of morals to a nineteen-year-old abused kid from a council house in Neyland.'

'Not necessarily.'

'Mostyn, I think the fact that I'm going to kill those two evil bastards tonight when you think I shouldn't demonstrates quite clearly that we don't have a similar moral understanding.'

'You should respect life, boy, regardless. Otherwise you're just a beast,' said Mostyn.

'Maybe so, Most, but I didn't create this beast! You know that. It's just not fucking fair you're all against me. I've risked my life tonight to fucking save you all!'

'We're not against you, son. We know those nasty pieces of work deserve justice. They can't get away with what they've done, the bastards. If you didn't show up tonight, who knows what might have happened. They say the only thing necessary for the triumph of evil is for just men to do nothing. You have done something tonight, Biscuits, something very brave, and I for one will always be truly grateful for your courage.'

Biscuits was moved, but determined. 'But they've still gotta go. Sorry, but they have.' He looked away and sucked down the last gulps of cider from his can.

'How are you going to kill them and get away with it and live happily ever after, you knobhead?' asked Jethro.

'Not quite sure yet, but a plan is coming together.' His drawn face turned back to Weird Head and Ronnie. They were now both on the floor. Ronnie was lying down, staring at the ceiling, still jabbering nonsense. Weird Head was sitting against the wall, staring straight ahead, miming into the universe. A piss stain darkened his lap.

Biscuits delved back into his rucksack and pulled out two half-litre bottles of cheap rum and a flask. He gave one bottle each to Weird Head and Ronnie, telling them it was an antidote to the madness. They drank them quickly and their bodies slunk lower.

'What are you doing, Biscuits? Just cut us free and let's go to the police,' pleaded Daisy.

'That's not going to work, Daisy. Sorry.' He pulled out another money bag from his jeans pocket and waved the small handful of blue tablets in their direction. 'They must be starving,' he grinned.

'Fucking hell, Biscuits, stop this shit. It's over. Just cut these fucking ropes.'

'Sorry, J.'

Biscuits turned around and approached Weird Head first. He whispered into his ear and helped him up off the floor. Biscuits picked up his flask from the table and wrapped his other arm around Weird Head, escorting him steadily out of the door like a hospital patient and out into the yard.

They continued to the edge of the bog where Biscuits had prepared the fire. The escarpment around them made Biscuits feel like he was inside the crater of a dormant volcano.

He sat Weird Head on a log, took out a lighter and lit the pieces of kindling. Soon the fire had caught and it began to crackle and roar. Biscuits continued his torment from the log opposite Weird Head, whispering at him to stay as close to the flames as possible. Spirits and ghosts didn't like flames – he was safe there.

Weird Head was sweating, his face just inches from them.

'I'm thirsty,' said Weird Head pathetically.

'No worries, Weird Head. I've got some hot coffee in my flask.' Biscuits leaned over and picked up the flask. He twisted off the cup, unscrewed the lid and poured a stream of steaming coffee. He rested it carefully on his knee as he took out the bag of blue pills and emptied eight of them onto the palm of his opposite hand. He counted them, smiled, and poured them straight into the cup of coffee. He took a twig from the grass and stirred for at least a minute while he stared flatly at Weird Head through the flames. Weird Head's massive face still shone with inner darkness, despite the fact that he was now a disabled, empty shell of a man.

Biscuits' heart raced. 'Here, Weird Head, drink this. It'll keep you warm.' He offered him the coffee.

Weird Head took it and within a few minutes the coffee was gone.

'Whatever you do, don't move. The volcano is alive with spirits,' Biscuits whispered.

'What? What volcano?' Weird Head looked up. Biscuits pointed upwards and dragged his finger along the ridge of the high escarpment that almost encircled them inside a rim of blackness. Weird Head's mouth dropped and his bottom lip began to quiver. He leaned in close to the flames, closed his eyes and began to mewl for his father.

Biscuits went back inside the house and bent down next to Ronnie's head. He whispered over him, 'Give me your arm, old toad. I'll help you down to the end of the road.'

Ronnie sat up. 'What does that mean?' he asked, innocent as a child.

'Eh? I didn't say anything.' Biscuits helped Ronnie to his feet and they both shuffled towards the door and out towards the fire on the moor.

'Coffee?' asked Biscuits.

No reply.

Biscuits emptied the remaining seven blue tablets into a fresh cup of coffee and gave it a good stir. He handed the cup over to Ronnie, who drank it down in one.

Ronnie was the first to die. It was quicker than he deserved. He'd been wailing for a couple of hours, screaming for the last forty minutes or so. But it was nice to finally have a bit of quiet, thought Biscuits, as he held Ronnie's head, face down, drowning him in the freezing brown bog water. He hardly struggled.

Weird Head couldn't react. He was still at one with the campfire, sat cross-legged like a villainous Buddha. Then the pain overwhelmed him too. Biscuits told him that the pains were the spirits that entered his head when he pulled away from the flames minutes earlier.

Weird Head tried to lean closer, his face twisted as the flames licked and singed his eyebrows and burned his cheeks. Biscuits stood up, tiptoed quietly behind Weird Head and placed his hands halfway down his thick back, then tipped him over his crossed legs into the fire. Weird Head's face and torso crashed onto the glowing timber, his hands seconds behind, his legs still tangled. His screams ignited pleas from inside the house that echoed out onto the moor as Weird Head's face began to melt in the flames. The smell of burning flesh made Biscuits gag. He quickly heaved Weird Head onto the spongy moorland grass. But it was too late – his face was scolded beyond recognition, his lips and eyelids had burned away, and the fabric of his jacket was smouldering into his skin. His tiny wails faded and faded in the few short minutes until he passed away.

Biscuits looked up to the sky and let out a dreadful noise – a limp roar that echoed across the farmyard, signalling to Mostyn, Jethro and

Daisy that it was all over.

In the distance, something caught Biscuits' eye. A lone figure walking across the dark moor with its hands in its pockets, its head down, coming towards him. Biscuits ran, tracking low, straight out into the bog, losing a shoe as he lay down flat, saturating the front of his clothes in the cold dank water.

The figure approached the fire. As it reached the bodies of Ronnie and Weird Head, Biscuits could see it was John the Ghost.

Biscuits remained still.

John looked organised. He pulled out a torch, put on some latex gloves and began to rearrange the bodies. He then went into the house.

Biscuits heard the commotion from inside as John entered.

John came back out carrying the empty cider cans and rum bottles and laid them randomly around Weird Head and Ronnie. He found the empty money bag, held it up to the flames and smirked when he saw the blue dust lining it. He tucked the bag into Ronnie's trouser pocket then searched the area carefully under the torchlight, picking up some of Biscuits' long hairs and sprinkling them nonchalantly into the last glowing embers of the fire. He looked out over the bog. Daybreak was approaching. 'Come on, Biscuits,' he shouted, 'it's time to go home now.'

Biscuits stood up, picked up his shoe and walked over to John.

'It's over now, son. All over.'

Biscuits dropped his head and they both walked slowly back towards the house.

Three days later, the shroud of fog lifted from the escarpment and a group of ramblers spotted the bodies of Weird Head and Ronnie on the moorland below.

A verdict of accidental death was reached. An overdose of lethal PMA was found in both Weird Head's and Ronnie's bodies, along with high doses of LSD and alcohol. The report concluded that Ronnie's drowning and Weird Head's burns were the result of their final desperate death throes as the toxic PMA killed them.

John the Ghost had wiped all traces of activity from the farmhouse after he'd helped Mostyn, Jethro, Daisy and Mr Price out. No line of suspicion was raised, probably in light of the notorious victims, and the case was closed.

John the Ghost broke into Weird Head's house the same day of his death to collect the old man, Weird Head's father. He came with no resistance, and, after a silent drive into town, John dropped him at the reception of Withybush A&E, then turned around, jumped back in his pick-up and vanished.

Epilogue

Mr Price spent two weeks in Withybush hospital, recovering from surgery to rebuild his throat. As soon as he was discharged, he went straight to Lewis Mill to see Mostyn. He offered a full and dignified apology, and handed Mostyn a bag containing eighty thousand pounds in cash. Mostyn accepted and the two old men made their peace and embraced. The next day, Mr Price announced his early retirement, sold his house and the abandoned farm and quietly, with the help of Mostyn, organised the repatriation of all of the machinery and tools to the farms they had been expropriated from.

Within weeks, Mr Price and Rosemary had relocated, without fuss or farewell, to Porthcawl, to see out their days.

Biscuits moved in with Boutros. His trauma was acute. Counselling was discussed, but they decided together to get away, to disappear for six months, to travel through India. Biscuits was excited. He wanted to go to Calcutta train station to see if maybe, just maybe, Anjali was still alive, sixteen years later.

Mostyn finally achieved his dream of extending his slurry pit.

Dragging her welly across the boot scrape, Ruth looked up and saw Jethro and Daisy pouring some pop at the kitchen sink.

'Alright, kids?' she asked.

They both smiled and nodded. 'Yep, fine, thanks,' said Jethro.

Daisy thought Ruth looked beautiful and elegant with her headscarf and rosy red lips.

Ruth was carrying a bundle of tomatoes from the greenhouse inside her turned-up jumper. 'Homemade bolognaise tonight, Most?'

'What's that? I'm not eating any of that foreign shit now, Ruth.'

Jethro and Daisy laughed.

'You'll eat what you're given, you ungrateful little toerag. It'll all be fresh and lovely, just food from the farm. How's that sound?'

'Alright, just don't put any of that curry in it.'

'Alright, just this time then. You're the boss.'

Daisy caught Ruth's eye and they shared a sneaky chuckle.

Jethro's heart warmed at Mostyn and Ruth's exchange. He

considered that maybe even his own mother may find happiness again one day.

'You sure you won't both come down after? It's a lovely evening,' said Daisy. 'The sunset's going to be magic, look.' She pointed to the cirrus clouds out west, steadily warming by the setting autumnal sun.

'No thanks, Dais,' said Mostyn. 'I promised the big man out there I'd take him fishing after supper.' Mostyn nodded at young Ted, busy picking worms from under the broken breeze-blocks on the back lawn.

Jethro smiled as he picked up the surfboard and headed out of the back door towards the Land Rover. 'Good luck!' he shouted.

'Aye, cheers, boy, might need that,' said Mostyn, shaking his head at the sight of Ted dipping a worm into his busy little mouth.

'Come on, boy,' shouted Mostyn, 'you gotta learn how to spool a reel before supper.'

'Coming,' the tiny voice yelled back.

As they strolled down towards the valley under the canopy of trees, Mostyn was reminded of the same fishing trips he'd taken with his grandfather over fifty years ago. They would just sit peacefully on the bank in the early evening heat, listening to the swish of small fish as they snapped through the surface of the river for the flies that hovered over it at dusk.

There was nothing peaceful about Ted. He was irate, unable to loop the worm onto the hook. Mostyn sighed and took over. He carefully double-hooked the wriggling earthworm onto the small black barb, leaving a good inch of its body dangling as juicy bait for the hungry sewin. The restless nature of the boy reminded Mostyn of Gareth – the constant frown interspersed with fits of laughter, never relaxed, always questioning, discovering.

They held the rod together and Mostyn gently swivelled their bodies to the right, then back, casting the line out over the silent river as it buzzed out of the reel.

'Wow, that was cool,' said Ted. 'So what do we do now?'

Mostyn sighed again and smiled. 'Well, my boy,' he said, taking off his tatty blazer. He laid it down on the scorched grass and sat carefully on top of it, crossing his legs. 'We're just gonna sit here, and wait.'

Jethro was sure that last wave was it.

Daisy was laughing.

'Don't fucking laugh, Dais. I nearly drowned then.'

'Yeah, whatever. Come on, let's paddle out a bit further, get your breath back.'

As Jethro paddled, the rolling motion of the swell made him tingle. This was some feeling, and it was natural. He sat up on his board and looked at the horizon, feeling microscopic but very real – a tiny blank space in the vastness. He didn't know where he was headed, where he should go, what would happen in the days ahead. He thought of Biscuits, now probably on a train tearing through the sultry plains of India with Boutros. He hoped they would return with Biscuits healed, at peace in himself, but he was not hopeful. How could a young man recover from those experiences? He didn't know.

He turned and looked across to Rickets Head, the resting phoenix, as majestic as ever. He thought of Mostyn. He imagined both of their bodies dropping off the cliffs, plummeting through the air, smashing onto the boulders below. They'd turned their backs on that precipice together.

He thought of Sparky, his ashes floating on the lonely water. Guilt still racked him. He could not put Biscuits' tirade in the farmhouse out of his mind. If Lewistock didn't happen, Sparky would still be alive.

Daisy paddled over and sat up on her board, close to Jethro. 'You alright, J?'

'I don't know.' He paused. He could see she too was holding back tears.

'Bad times don't last, J. We'll be stronger for them. My dad said we have to grow with the troubles, and that we can never forget them. Everything is a gift from the universe, the positive and the negative. Happiness will come back soon, my love, and we'll be ready to rock.'

Daisy wiped her eyes, wrapped her arms around Jethro's shoulders and kissed him tenderly. The realness of it flicked a switch inside Jethro. He had Daisy, Mostyn, the land and the sea. He was alive, today.

'Quick, there's a set coming,' said Daisy.

Jethro looked out at the thin shadows of the approaching waves stacking against the orange sky. His mind contracted back into the moment. He paddled with his hands, rotating his big board to face the shore. He glanced up onto the pebbles. A couple with two young boys caught his eye. They were rummaging in a picnic hamper and pointing out to sea, watching the surfers. Jethro smiled. He lay down on his board and began to paddle.

Acknowledgements

Thank you: Julie, Maria, Mark, Matt, Meady, Tanya, Terence and Vicky for reading and for conversations. Nan, for stories of times past. David Wilson Photography for inspiration. Particular thanks to my mentor, Laurence King. Most of all, Jess and the boys, and Mum and Dad.

richardwilliamsbooks.com

Richard Williams

Richard Williams was raised on a dairy farm in north Pembrokeshire. Following a degree and masters degree in Development Studies from Exeter University and LSE respectively, Richard worked as a technical writer at the newly-created Global Fund to fight HIV/AIDS, TB and Malaria.

His later success in the restaurant industry has been balanced in recent years with creative writing courses with Anjali Joseph (UEA) and his current mentor, Daren King. *Mostyn Thomas and the Big Rave* is his first novel.

Graffeg Fiction

Down The Road and Round The Bend by Roy Noble

In this collection of twenty short tales, Roy Noble celebrates the fascinating histories and traditional stories rooted in Wales, some canonical, and others less well-known today but equally deserving of attention. Seamlessly blending anecdote and personal insight with historical detail, Roy has compiled a selection of humorous and engrosing explorations of traditional Wales spanning the length and breadth of the country.

Praise for Roy Noble:

'...he seems unerringly to know every yard on every road in Wales. He presses mental buttons and comes up with a story, a memory or a reflection about every community he has ever called in or driven through.' MICHAEL BOON, WESTERN MAIL

'Many uplifting tales that had me laughing out loud' DENNIS GETHIN, PRESIDENT OF THE WELSH RUGBY UNION

£8.99, ISBN 9781912050178

The Offline Project by Dan Tyte

The internet defines Gerard Kane. But after a dumping and a death in the family, can going off-grid save him?

His pursuit of something outside his smartphone takes him from his Welsh home to a new community in the Danish woodland. Here, Gerard is able to share his new ideal of an offline existence with a community of former internet addicts, but life in this new world may be more sinister than it appears.

Dan Tyte's debut novel, *Half Plus Seven*, was published by Parthian in 2014. He has performed at the Hay Festival, Southbank Centre, and Edinburgh Fringe, and is a regular commentator on BBC Radio Wales. His short story Onwards is frequently taught at the American University of Paris.

£8.99, ISBN 9781912213702

Graffeg Books

The Most Glorious Prospect:
Garden Visiting In Wales 1639-1900 by Bettina Harden
Hardback, 250 x 250mm, 256 pages, £30.00
ISBN: 9781910862629

The Owl Book by Jane Russ
Hardback, 150 x 150mm, 160 pages, £9.99
ISBN: 9781912050420

Lost Lines of Wales: Bangor to Afon Wen
by Paul Lawton and David Southern
Hardback 150 x 200mm, 64 pages, £8.99
ISBN: 9781912213115

Lost Lines of Wales: Rhyl To Corwen
by Paul Lawton and David Southern
Hardback, 150 x 200mm, 64 pages, £8.99
ISBN: 9781912213108

The Offline Project by Dan Tyte
Paperback, 216 x 138mm, 280 pages, £8.99
ISBN: 9781912213702

A Year In Pembrokeshire
by Jamie Owen and David Wilson
(Publication June 2018)
Hardback, 200 x 200mm, 192 pages, £20.00
ISBN: 9781912213658

Lost Tramways of Wales: Cardiff by Peter Waller
(Publication June 2018)
Hardback, 150 x 200mm, 64 pages, £8.99
ISBN: 9781912213122

Lost Tramways of Wales: North Wales by Peter Waller
(Publication June 2018)
Hardback, 150 x 200mm, 64 pages, £8.99
ISBN: 9781912213139

Lost Tramways of Wales: South Wales and Valleys
by Peter Waller (Publication June 2018)
Hardback, 150 x 200mm, 64 pages, £8.99
ISBN: 9781912213146

Lost Tramways of Wales: Swansea and Mumbles
by Peter Waller (Publication June 2018)
Hardback, 150 x 200mm, 64 pages, £8.99
ISBN: 9781912213153

Mostyn Thomas and The Big Rave
by Richard Williams (Publication October 2018)
Paperback, 216 x 138mm, 224 pages, £8.99
ISBN 9781912654161

For a full list of Graffeg titles and to place an order, please
visit our website: www.graffeg.com.

Graffeg Children's Books

The Pond by Nicola Davies and Cathy Fisher
Hardback, 250 x 250mm, 36 pages, £11.99
ISBN: 9781912050703

The Snow Leopard by Jackie Morris
Hardback, 365 x 270mm, 24 pages, £17.99
ISBN: 9781912050475

The Ice Bear by Jackie Morris
Hardback, 365 x 270mm, 24 pages, £17.99
ISBN: 9781912050468

Bertram Likes To Sew by Karin Celestine
Hardback, 150 x 150mm, 48 pages, £6.99
ISBN: 9781912213610

The Very Silly Dog by Nick Cope
Paperback, 150 x 150mm, 48 pages, £4.99
ISBN: 9781912213511

No I Don't Wanna Do That by Nick Cope
Paperback, 150 x 150mm, 48 pages, £4.99
ISBN: 9781912213535

For a full list of Graffeg children's titles and to place an order, please visit our website: www.graffeg.com.